A M
TH

Wenatchi Werebears

EMMA ALISYN
FIERCELY REAL ROMANCE

Mate for the Bear
Copyright © 2015 Emma Alisyn

For information contact :
www.hardcandiespublishing.com

Cover and Interior design by Emma Alisyn
Book Formatting by Derek Murphy @Creativindie
ISBN: 978-0692693650

First Edition: 2015

*Please feel free to color the book plate on
the following page.*

*For more coloring designs by Emma Alisyn
visit www.hardcandiespublishing.com*

Live to Color, Color to Live

This Book Belongs To:

CHAPTER ONE

"You look lovely," her mother said, gliding a comb through Annina's long tail of coffee brown hair. It hung down her back, glossy from an entire can of olive oil spray.

She'd overdone it just a little.

Annina turned and took her mother's hands. "Mother. Stop fussing."

The older female's summer brown face crumpled, then smoothed as she struggled to contain her emotions.

"My baby. You're so young- I don't like using you this way."

She would always be young to her mother. "It would be an insult not to present him with a high ranked daughter from our Clan."

Mother sighed. "I want better for you. A love match. A mate, maybe, and cubs. Not to be used as a concubine for the sake of old tradition."

"Not tradition's sake. The Clan's survival."

Because if the Blade's had their way, in the next council meeting Fire Eagle land would be taken and their fishing rights along with it. If that happened, the Clan would be destitute.

They lived in a hub of land, trading the aggravation of neighbors for sharing rich resources. Most Clan's occupied a single territory, but these lands were old, and many Bears had settled there over the years. Long years, full of fighting over dens and hunting rights.

Fishing rights to the Wenatchi River wild salmon brought her Clan money, and prestige in the Territory Council. The voices of Fire Eagle Elders held weight because much of their wealth they redistributed, gaining votes of those Clans less fortunate. The Blade's wanted that voice- wanted that power. And because Grandfather's mismanagement had led to an...

interruption of some of the usual redistribution, their weakening position allowed enemies an opportunity Annina couldn't let come to fruition.

If it meant presenting herself for The Bear's pleasure, if it meant bearing The Bear's cub with the possibility that mother and cub would be tossed out on their backside once the archaic year and day obligation was over, then that was what she would do.

So at the Welcoming tonight when the Clans presented their bright, beautiful daughters, Fire Eagle would present theirs. Not quite as beautiful, but certainly with a unique enough look of her own. Or so Grandfather insisted.

Her mother left Annina alone. She stood in her room staring out the window, smoothing hands down curving hips, recalling times in the history of their people when plump had been a sign of a Clan's wealth and a female's ability to carry healthy cubs for her mate. Now the ideal followed the human trend of boyish slimness- but Annina refused to believe that any real man would want to hold a fleshless simulacra in his arms at night when he could have chest, ass, and hips overflowing his arms.

She'd never been insecure about her more voluptuous figure like some of her cousins. She chose clothing to accentuate her natural curves. When she finally let a male undress her for the first time, he would be undressing an original Earth Goddess, a real female designed to reward a mate after a hard day's work. A female he could pillow his head on.

She used the window as a mirror and slathered her full mouth in neutral gloss, dusted a bit of shimmer over her high cheekbones and along the bridge of a regal nose.

"Annina, the car is ready," her mother called from the bottom of the stairs.

She turned from the window, picking up the dress laid over her bed. It was long, one shouldered and draped modestly over her chest, nipping in at the waist and flowing to her ankles. At mid thigh the opaque fabric became sheer, revealing shapely legs set to advantage by high heels. She was already a tall girl; the heels would add an extra four inches. She smiled. Annina knew, from the brief her grandfather's male had provided, that the new Bear was tall and didn't particularly care for petite females. It gave her hope. Though she wasn't classically beautiful, Annina knew her thigh length hair pleased shifters, along with wide dark eyes with slightly slanted tips.

Taking a deep breath, she distanced herself emotionally from her family, from the side of herself that was warm, funny, and a little playful. When she opened her eyes, she was Fire Eagle's best secret weapon.

The Bear sent to them was not from the elder Clans.

Because Annina didn't know his Clan, she didn't know his attributes. Would he admire strength and cunning, or demure innocence? She knew she'd gathered the best information on him possible- her informants among the others had assured her of that, but she didn't know enough about him to make more than an educated guess.

What she did know was that he was a silent presence in the regional Council. A junior member, for sure, but a member nonetheless. He'd worked his way through the ranks based on a reputation for shrewdness and unwavering loyalty once his word was given- but he was also known to be swift to retaliate against lawbreakers. The Council was sending him to their battling territory because he couldn't be bought, or embroiled in their already messy politics. He had no existing ties or loyalties that might sway him towards one clan against another.

Knowing all this, Annina had already decided that straightforward honesty would be the best approach. An old-fashioned seduction. He would want a companion, an advisor from the territory who he could trust. She hoped.

The formal Welcoming would be held outside under the midnight moon as was custom, but the lodge was already set up with a spread of delicacies, her Clan's spicy smoked salmon among them. A bounty would be laid before Bear, to prove the territory was wealthy, its resources abundant. They all smarted from knowing the Council had deemed their infighting dangerous enough to require an overlord- when they'd gone for decades governing themselves. But Annina supposed it was time- they'd been left to fend for themselves for too long and many had forgotten that there was an authority over all North American shifters- an authority they must bow to, whether they remembered or not.

She spotted several other family heads, along with the daughters they would present, each hoping to capture the Bear for the year and day term. Annina would be the only representative from her Clan present and figured she could work that to her advantage. She made sure to stand a little away from the others, allowing a bubble of stillness to encase her. The stark red of her gown shimmered against her dusky skin and the forest provided a dramatic backdrop. If she thought too hard, she realized she felt like a poser. At what other time in her life would she be worried about how trees looked next to her dress?

The Bear entered; Kavanaugh. The only title he would be given in this territory. They were all bear, but he would be Bear, over them all. A murmur ran through the crowd and when Annina saw why, she nearly laughed. Though this was a formal black and white affair- ridiculous for a midnight forest gathering among native people- he wore a thin blue sweater and jeans. A V neck revealed a glimpse of smooth, hard chest underneath, the fabric clinging to broad shoulders in a way that left nothing to imagination.

Head slowly turning to survey the crowd, his amber eyes glittering, he tucked a lock of wavy light brown hair behind an ear. Annina studied the angular bones of his face, the tilted shape of his eyes and bronze of his skin.

Blade headed the ceremonies- lengthy speeches welcoming him to the territory. Proclamations of loyalty and retellings of the oldest tales that honored the strength of Bear. Songs were sung to the beat of drums and finally, when she'd thought her patience was at an end, the Clans presented their daughters for his perusal.

The females paraded in front of him, one by one. Coy, slender young girls with slim hips and subtle breasts- and if they were all of age, she would eat her earrings- and statuesque, bold glamazons with heaving chests and hips made to birth cubs. He made all the right sounds, was perfectly courteous. But she watched his eyes, saw how his eyes moved around the crowd, restless. Saw the tapping of his fingers before he caught himself.

Every Clan had presented a member for his choosing, but she had yet to walk forward as Fire Eagle's choice, swallowing ire that her territory still abided by this outdated custom. Her instinct told her to wait until the ebb and flow of his attention was optimal. A few times her heart stopped as she saw a brief spark of interest light his eyes- and thought she had waited too long. But no, he would nod, dismiss the girl. Watch again, impassively, as another took her place.

After all the females presented themselves, he lifted a hand, bringing the gathering back to silence. She moved through the crowd then, placing herself in a position where at the right time she could gain his notice.

"Your daughters are beautiful," he said, expression impassive. "I am not worthy."

Annina couldn't help herself; her laugh rang out in response to his stoic, ridiculous claim. The ridiculousness of *that* bit of pompousness put her at ease.

Every eye turned on her. A lesser female would have frozen, especially when the arctic eyes of the Bear settled on her, fey and thoughtful. She walked forward, a small smile playing about her lips. Years of training allowed her to move with greater than average shifter grace- a litheness she accentuated now.

Halting in front of him, she willed him to see her- young, brazen, sensual. A female encased in silk ready to be peeled away for his pleasure. Intelligence and strength in her eyes, as well as an unwillingness to fully submit. She willed him to see it- to see a mate ready to match him.

"Do you find me amusing?" Bear asked. Rather than a gauche growl, his voice dropped to a low purr. His voice brushed against her like warm velvet, a rough lap on skin already sensitized under his gaze. She inhaled, drawing herself together.

She sank into a perfect curtsy, only half mocking. "No, Eldest. I doubt that you're unworthy."

"You're pert. What Clan are you?"

Rising, she held his eyes. "I am Annina, Eldest. Clan Fire Eagle."

"Annina." He drew the name out, rolling the syllables around his tongue, making the name sound exotic. A finger reached out, brushing the line of her cheek with the lightness of butterfly wings. His scent filled her nostrils; she leaned in, taking him into her lungs. "So you think you're what I seek?"

"I think you need a consort in this territory willing to place your interests above her own."

He smiled, the expression both dark and intimate. For a moment, she forgot she was predator pretending to be prey.

"And you're willing to place me above your Clan- above yourself?"

Annina dared take one step closer to him than protocol dictated, breaking into the circle of his personal space. Allowing him to feel the heat and promise of her body. He looked down at her, utterly still.

"Ask me in the morning, Eldest, and you'll have an answer for yourself."

He did not release her from his gaze. "Then come."

CHAPTER TWO

Annina accepted Kavanaugh's outstretched hand, watching the furious faces of her enemies as he escorted her into the lodge.

"You're not taking me to your cave?" she asked, eyebrow arching as she tested his temperament

"Not quite yet." He glanced down at her, a small smile in cool eyes, not seeming to mind her small opening flirtation. "A bite of something to eat first, hmm?" His knuckle brushed the line of her cheek. "We wouldn't want you to fade away into nothing."

Annina grinned. "I hope that wasn't a fat joke."

He blinked, head tilting. Annina realized he only topped her by a few inches; they were well matched, at least in height.

"I'm teasing," she said, having mercy on him. After all, what male would know how to respond to that? There really was no right answer. He grimaced, a slip in his mask that delighted her. She laughed, allowing her expression to soften, open for him. Drawing him in.

"I confess, I don't enjoy formal events," she said, lowering her eyes to the ground as they walked to the tables. "I'm a bit... shy."

"You're a bit of a liar."

They approached the buffet, Annina ignoring the sounds of people gathering behind them. No one would approach the tables until Bear and his female had filled their plates, but they pressed as close as they dared.

"Let's get you fed, hmm? I wouldn't want anyone to think I can't take care of what is mine."

The thrill up her spine puzzled Annina- her feminine nature reacting to the hint of possessiveness in his tone. He picked up a plate, placing savory pieces of lamb and vegetables on the white porcelain. Choosing saffron rice with plump golden raisins soaked in wine. Baked, honeyed apples and decadent chocolate cake. Fresh sliced fruit. And salmon. Plenty of salmon. A feast.

"I hope you like fish," she said, watching him choose. "You'll get plenty of it here. We even put it in the desserts."

He paused, eyebrow twitching.

"Salmon meringue pie," she murmured, pointing to a selection of cheeses. He obliged, artfully arranging bite sized pieces on her plate. "Don't knock it until you try it. I should be serving you, not the other way around, you know."

"I waited tables when I was younger," he replied, moving to a selection of beverages. "Service will always be a bit of a habit. Wine?"

"I'd rather not. I prefer to keep my wits about me." He chose a small bottle of sparkling water. "I always thought a year in some kind of customer service employment should be mandatory to be considered an adult. That way more people learn a bit of civility."

He smiled briefly. "It is harder to be rude when you've been on the other side."

Annina studied him, studied the plate he'd made her. "You did well. I couldn't have made myself a better selection."

"I think that's a good sign."

She turned back to the buffet, analyzing the various dishes and then reached for a plate.

"What are you doing?" he asked.

"I'm going to return the favor, and see how well I choose."

He looked amused, but took a step back in willingness to play along. She liked the way his loose hair brushed his shoulders in nut-brown waves, not confined or braided.

Well, the obvious choice would be to go for the steak, or to flaunt her Clan's salmon, but instead she chose small portions of traditional dishes, things he wouldn't find anywhere but in this territory, among her people. Flaky whitefish prepared in sprigs of freshly picked herbs indigenous to the surrounding land. Mushrooms and wild greens, a small bowl of venison stew spiked with dried berries that were poisonous if not prepared properly. A sweet corn cake drizzled in local honey.

"Interesting choices," he said when she was done, topping the entire plate with a hunk of flat bread. "Why no meat?"

"You don't walk with the bluster of a red meat eater. There's fish, though. Do you want to try some of the sauces?"

"No, I don't like to cover up the natural flavor of my food."

A long table was set up with a place set aside for Kavanaugh and his chosen, but he indicated she should follow him back outside, choosing a tree stump on the outer rim of the gathering circle big enough for them to share.

Annina arched an eyebrow as she sat, carefully arranging her skirt under her so it wouldn't snag. "Don't like eating with an audience?"

"Hmmm. How will I fish out all your secrets unless I have you to myself?"

She brushed a finger across the back of his palm. "I no longer have any secrets- not from you, anyway."

Kavanaugh's shimmering gold eyes remained impassive. "Everyone has secrets, Annina. And a female's secrets are the most dangerous of them all."

Something stirred underneath his expression and she shivered, remembering she was dealing with Bear.

"I won't have my mother saying I must have been raised by wolves," she murmured, spreading a linen napkin over her lap before she began to eat.

She passed him the other cloth wrapped setting she'd snagged on the way out, noticing that he seemed to prefer to use his fingers, and wondered again what Clan he hailed from. He ate gracefully, with the air of someone who was used to doing so. She thought it interesting he'd want to eat under the moonlight, alone. It spoke to her of a romantic streak, perhaps unacknowledged. Or at least a personality that didn't require the limelight or constant acknowledgment from others of his power and authority.

"The white fish is good," he said. "But you didn't give me any of the smoked salmon."

He eyed her plate and Annina had to laugh. Just like a man. Always wanting something he didn't have.

"I didn't want to boast," she said. "Try some."

He reached for a piece on her plate, responding to her invitation. She slapped his wrist, a lighting quick movement. He was just as fast, grabbing her wrist in an instinctive reaction, then releasing her, slowly, when she didn't move. Violence scented the air, just a hint.

"Allow me, Eldest," she said, holding his narrowed eyes with her own, a small smile on her lips. Annina picked up the piece of salmon, bringing it slowly to his lips. It hovered there a second before he opened his mouth, allowing her to place it, delicately, between his two lips. He took the morsel, chewing slowly, allowing her to feed him another piece.

"Is it good?"

"Very flavorful," he said. "It has a kick."

"We use a special blend of spices. The heat lingers on the palate. I don't think the wine you chose will go well with this, though."

Picking up his glass, she took a sip, rolling the wine around her mouth and allowing the crisp apple to coat her tongue and lips.

"Well?" he asked.

Annina leaned forward. "Judge for yourself."

She brushed her lips against his, opening her mouth to nip at his bottom lip, asking him to indulge her. His mouth opened and her tongue slid in, seeking his own. He was still but for the play of their lips on one another. She tasted the smoky spicy fish as well as the wild greens he'd eaten. After a moment in which she felt their tension begin to rise, she pulled away.

"Well?" Annina asked. "How do you judge?"

"I think it goes well. An unlikely pairing, but oddly... fitting. A strong combination of flavors, no doubt."

"Strength is found in unexpected pairings." She reached up, twined a lock of his hair around her finger. "Times are dangerous, disputes turn savage. Men plot and greed holds sway over honor. Eat." Heat crept into her voice, a promise, one she increasingly anticipated fulfilling. "You'll need all your strength this night."

Loud voices approached, an angry male answered by the hard tones of another. Annina rose, recognizing the storm. Anticipating it. Kavanaugh stepped to her side, glancing briefly when she shifted to flank him at his left, slightly behind.

Terrence Blade, head of the Clan that pushed the most to terminate her families fishing rights, strode towards them, another male at his heels. A shifter obviously not from the territory, with short pale hair and nearly colorless eyes.

"This moron insists on speaking to you, Kavanaugh," the stranger said, voice low and rough, accented in a way she didn't recognize. "You told me to be nice tonight. This is me being nice and not smashing his ass for being a pain."

"Like you could, you pale faced flunky," Blade said, lip curled.

Terrence had presented his eldest daughter for the Bear's pleasure. A lovely girl, petite and doe eyed with a cloud of curly red brown hair. And not even out of high school yet. But then, Annina was surprised Terrence even bothered letting the child go, considering his views on educating females beyond the kitchen and gardens.

"Good evening, Terrence," she purred. "I'm sorry, did you need something? Your daughter looked so lovely tonight, by the way."

He rushed her. Or tried. She didn't blink; they were such old enemies it was almost his way of showing friendship.

"Zeke," Kavanaugh said.

Zeke was ahead of him, though. Annina watched in interest as he intercepted Blade with a quick move, pinning him to the ground in a hold with his arms twisted at an awkward angle.

"Get off me!"

"You attack your master?" Zeke asked, voice chilled.

"Not him, you stupid Nord, the bitch at his side." His feet drummed into the ground. Amazing; though Zeke's muscles flexed with strain, he held Terrence fast, jaw set. Annina studied him, mentally calculating the family finances. A man with the skills to restrain rather than kill and the judgment to know when a situation called for one over the other...that was a valuable soldier.

"Ah. Bear's woman. Well, in that case…" He twisted. Blade yowled.

Kavanaugh sighed. "Zeke."

"Are you going to behave, cub, or do I break your arms?"

"I won't hurt her," he sneered. "Now let me up."

When Terrence rose to his feet under Zeke's watchful eye, Annina spoke

"I'd like to offer you a position with the Fire Eagle."

Kavanaugh's head whipped towards her, eyes widening. "What?"

"My family is the richest landowner in this territory." Zeke rocked back on his heels. "I'll double whatever you're being paid."

"Are you trying to poach my guard?" Kavanaugh asked, disbelief shading his voice.

She glanced at him, apologetically. "It's just business, Eldest. You understand. He's magnificent. My Clan needs someone like him and we're rich, after all."

"Oh, yeah?" Zeke looked at Kavanaugh, eyebrow raised. "How rich?"

She began to answer his question when Terrence interrupted. "I didn't come here for this." He fixed his angry glare on Bear, straightened his tux. "I demand a second choosing."

"On what grounds?" Annina asked, temper rising in her throat. Her thighs tensed- she wanted to jump him. A small growl slipped past her throat, forcing her to rein herself in. Smashing him wouldn't help her family. Not yet, anyway.

"If we had known the Bear preferred his women old and fat, we would have presented a female accordingly."

Annina just laughed. If over twenty-one was considered old, it just proved what a chauvinist Terrence was. The word fat- well, she couldn't argue with the pejorative term. She preferred curvy, however. Kavanaugh stiffened, obviously not liking the implied insult.

"We weren't given a fair chance," Blade insisted.

"Fire Eagle presented a choice to my liking," Kavanaugh said. "I will not do a second choosing. If you don't like it, you know what you can do."

Stop whining and go home, Annina wanted to say- but knew the last thing Kavanaugh needed was a female who picked fights or aggravated an already tense situation. She'd probably have to learn to keep her mouth shut... more often.

Terrence glared at her. Glaring at Bear would be a challenge- it was safer to take his ire out on her, or at least he might think so.

She smiled sweetly. "Don't worry, Blade. I'll put in a good word for you."

After Zeke escorted him away Kavanaugh looked at her. "You'll put in a good word?"

Annina pulled her loose hair over one shoulder, drawing his eyes to the silky strands. "I couldn't help it. His family has been a thorn in my Clan's claw for decades."

He studied her. "There's a story there."

"A boring one. Especially with dinner getting cold."

Kavanaugh sighed. "This is going to be interesting."

"You have *no* idea."

They spoke of small things over dinner, tacitly agreeing to steer around bigger things. Some of the conversation was amusing, some grave. She asked him about his childhood- funny stories, childish hurts. She wanted to know the male, get a glimpse of his inner world. Determine how best to approach the subject of the Boon.

She was surprised when he did it for her.

After they'd set aside their plates, he looked at her, eyes half lidded. It was the look of a male ready to pounce, as if he were strategizing how to seduce her, as she strategized how to seduce him. The calculation in his eyes thrilled her, both because she enjoyed the challenged and because she knew she would also enjoy the chase. Annina found herself falling into the courting dance in a way she hadn't anticipated. She had wanted to remain above feeling, above desire- above just being a female with a male- because she had a job to do and people who depended on her. She couldn't allow her emotions to make her weak or soften her thinking.

"Why did you offer yourself?" he asked. "How am I worthy of Fire Eagle's first daughter?"

"I think it's rather a matter of my worth, not yours."

"I'm not foolish enough to think so," he replied, eyes cool. "Female, don't toy with me. What will you ask for your Boon?"

Annina studied him. Traditionally a Boon was granted the morning after, when the Bear was well satisfied. In fact, she had counted on that, needing every edge she could get if she was to ask him to begin his tenure by starting a war with one of the most powerful clans in the territory. Leaning closer, she touched his hand, idly caressing the backs of his fingers.

"Eldest, will you trust me?" she asked. "Allow us to just be tonight. The morning is soon enough to speak of Boons."

The hand she caressed rose, cupped the back of her neck in a grip both gentle and unyielding. "I prefer to know the price of pleasure before I imbibe."

She turned her head slightly, aware he let her. Kissed his wrist. "I will be with you, at your side, in your bed, for a year and a day. I would not ask you anything against your interests."

He considered. Annina watched him thinking, saw the decision in his face.

"Alright. Will you come home with me?"

She leaned back on her hands, teasing him with a slow, sensuous smile, her eyes smoldering. Strands of her hair spilled from his fingers as he released her.

"Why not feast here, Eldest? The forest holds no danger for you."

Kavanaugh rose to his feet, expression inscrutable. "I don't want anyone to hear my female's screams. Those are for me alone."

CHAPTER THREE

Kavanaugh had taken residence in a vacation cabin, beautifully restored, a few miles away from the lodge. It suited him, and she approved of the distance it placed between him and other people. Most of the Clan families still lived in town, though a few still preferred to make the mountains their home.

Wood floors gleamed, offsetting warm colored walls. Furniture was minimal, dark, and comfortable looking. Mainly leather pieces with brightly colored throw pillows. She saw plenty of books and a few pieces of art on the wall, obviously one of a kind and hung with care. Annina wondered how long he had been in town- the place looked fully unpacked and almost lived in.

She'd touched him on the way to his home. Brief touches with her fingers, whispery soft, long looks under her lashes and suggestive taunts. All designed to enflame not only his body, but also his mind.

He led her up a set of stairs- herded her really. Opening a door from behind her, he nudged her into a masculine bedroom. Lush neutral carpet and a low platform bed completed the room's decor. Annina stared, brow rising. She'd seen minimal- but this was *minimal*.

"Maybe I can-"

"Quiet." Two hands placed themselves on her back and shoved.

She stumbled towards the bed, and then turned, glaring. His eyes were blazing, the calm mask gone.

"So you like to tease?" he asked, voice a silky croon as he stalked her. "I'll take payment for every giggle out of your flesh."

"I don't giggle."

Annina began to realize she'd taunted a beast. Bear loomed over her sprawled body, no mercy in his eyes, shoulders set with every intent to devour her flesh whether she willed it or no. He covered her with his body, hands planted on either side of her head. She eyed his bunched arms, wanting to see the bare flesh if he was going to show off for her.

"You're wearing too many clothes," she said, wrapping a hand around the back of his neck. She drew him down to her mouth, nipping at his lips.

He kissed her, opening her lips with an intensity that sent thrills up and down her spine. She unbuttoned his shirt as his tongue pushed into her mouth, playing with her. Teeth grazed her lips. Sharp teeth. Annina opened her eyes, knowing the amber glow of his iris echoed hers. Pulling the shirt off his shoulders, she ran her hands over his chest, feeling the cut of his abs and pecs. She appreciated that he wasn't smooth, but allowed his natural fine dusting of hair to remain.

Unsnapping his pants, pushing inside silky boxers to palm his cock, Annina smiled when he hissed, mouth traveling to her neck, teeth sinking into her flesh for a moment before he let go.

His hands rose, pushing hers away. "Take off the dress before I rip it away from you."

Kavanaugh gave her enough room to move, rising to his feet and stepping back. Annina sat up, reaching behind her for the zipper of the gown, peeling the cloth from her flesh slowly, revealing her ample breasts an inch at a time. The dress came with a built in bra- that barely supported her, but she'd never heard any male complain of overflowing breasts- so she hadn't worn one. The gown pooled at her waist, the heavy globes of her breasts swinging free for his perusal. Firm, dusky with rosy brown nipples, she lifted the weight of them in her hands, pressing them together to tease him with the shape, size, and cleavage that came along with being an extra curvy girl.

Bear stepped forward, sliding his hands underneath hers, hefting the weight, and massaging her flesh. She closed her eyes, head tilting back as his fingers plucked her nipples, causing a shudder to shimmer through her body. Each tug of her nipples connected to her clit, warming and jarring it to life. When she felt his mouth close around one breast, she nearly cried out, back arching, encouraging his play with her flesh.

His hands wrapped around her waist and he tugged her to her feet long enough to push the dress into a puddle on the floor. Fingers hooked into the flimsy ribbon ties of her panties and yanked, tearing the scrap of lace from her body so she stood before him completely bare, save for the heels. Which, of course, he didn't touch.

Burnished eyes roved over her body, and if it weren't for the heat of his regard and the cock dripping glistening drops of liquid, she would have thought from his hard expression that he found her wanting.

"Let me take you in my mouth," Annina said, making a move to drop to her knees.

He stopped her, holding her still before he dropped to his knees before her.

"No," Kavanaugh said. "First I want to eat out this pussy. Lick you until you cum."

The words jolted her, liquid pooling between her thighs. Annina licked dry lips. "Well, then. Age before beauty."

He froze for a second, eyes spearing her, and then sharp teeth flashed, a wolfish grin- for a Bear.

When she felt the rasp of his tongue on her slit, her knees nearly buckled. Imprisoning arms around her knees kept her upright as he licked and tormented her clit, pushing her thighs further apart and spreading her labia with his fingers to give himself better access.

"Oh, God." Her breath was broken, speech beyond a few syllables impossible.

His tongue flicked against her clit in a fast, rhythmic motion that drew pleasure out of her like a reverse vortex. Pressure grew, concentrating into throbbing mass of nerves she thought might send her mad. It was torture- a need for release she knew only he could assuage. When she thought she might start to go mad, he rose. Annina nearly swore at him, feeling the prickle of claws under her nails, a rumbling in her chest. He laughed at her, dark and sensuous, the laugh of a male who knew full well the torture he inflicted.

Annina tore at the rest of his clothes and he let her, pushing her back onto the bed when he was finally completely naked. She took a deep breath, struggled to control her ire that he'd deliberately left her unfinished, greedily taking in the honed muscular body and smooth bronze skin. He leaned back over her, dominance in every line of his body.

"Tell me how to please you," she said, running her hands up and down his back. His pleasure equaled her own. His tongue lapped at her nipples and she gasped. She hooked a leg around his waist; her hand was around his cock, caressing the hard length as she looked up at him, dark hair falling around his shoulders.

"Do you want me to fuck you?" he purred. "Take this juicy pussy until you scream?"

Her lip pulle dup in a snarl. "Enough games, Kavanuagh."

He took her leg from around his waist, draped it over his shoulder, did the same with her other leg. The angle was tight for her body, but she realized with him standing it gave his cock optimal access. The bulbous head nudged her entrance, sliding inside an inch at a time. She gasped, biting her lip to keep from crying out.

"Tight," he said, voice strained.

Annina whimpered, hands burying themselves in the sheet. He continued to push inside her, the walls of her pussy slowly adjusting around him, slowly accepting the invasion. The fullness was incredible, a possession she hadn't imagined when she'd experimented by inserting her own fingers in the deep recesses of night, dreaming about what sex would be like.

When his cock bumped against the head of her hymen, he paused, eyes narrowing. "You're a virgin."

She nodded. "I've been busy."

A snort of laughter, amber irises bright. "Then you're all mine."

He pushed through the barrier, finally wrenching the held back cry from her throat, sheathing himself to the hilt.

Sweetly, unexpectedly, he took her lips in a gentle kiss, murmuring, "I won't move until you're ready."

Annina wrapped her arms around his neck. "Take me."

She didn't have to tell him twice. He withdrew, and then slammed into her again, watching her face as he began to fuck her with a single-minded intensity that bordered on ruthless. He herded her relentlessly towards pleasure, expertly took his own in return, pounding into her with the strength of Bear, her breasts jiggling in time to his heavy thrusts. Soon she could no longer hold back her cries, moaning and whimpering and screaming when his hips hit a spot inside her that sent shards of electricity throughout her body.

When the climax overtook her it was as if he had picked her up and thrown her bodily over a cliff, sending her plummeting into a shock of icy and hot water beneath. Waves crashed over her, stealing her breath, wracking her body in helpless shudders. Hot, sticky seed filled her as he came. He pulled out of her several moments later, pulling her onto her side in a cradle.

"I'm going to have my way with you again," she said, voice slightly slurred from the pleasure.

He laughed softly, kissed her shoulder. "Who took whom, hmm?"

The scent of sex blooming in her nostrils, their mingled juices smeared on her thighs, Annina felt his warmth and pleasure in her mind, the surprise and hopefulness for the future mingled with satisfaction and possessiveness. Sleepily, she shared her own hope and-

She reared up, stiffening. Twisted to stare down at him with shock. His pupils were dilated as he returned her expression.

"My God." She didn't know who spoke, him or her. But the next thing she knew she was on her back, Kavanaugh looming over her with narrowed eyes. His presence in her mind was gone as if a door had slammed shut.

"Did you do that?" he demanded.

She laughed, a little dazed, hand rising to her throbbing head. "Eldest, I'm no sorcerer."

He stared at her. "Do you realize what that was?"

She shook her head. "Really cosmic fucking?"

He swore, rolling to his feet. "No, you silly child. That was the beginning of a mate bond."

She perched herself on one elbow. "Why, Eldest, this is so sudden."

"It's not a joke."

"No." Her tone was practical rather than placating, sleepy satiation rapidly disappearing as reality crashed down. Annina realized he'd have to be handled with care. No male like to feel trapped, or shocked by a sudden bond. "But if it is a mate bond, there isn't anything we can do about it. Sometimes they don't fully manifest."

Kavanaugh's expression slid from angry to inscrutable. "You're right. There's nothing to get excited over."

She wasn't sure how to take that. "Oh, really?" She rolled away, rising to her feet. "Thank you for a lovely evening. I'll-"

Arms wrapped around her waist, tumbling her back onto the bed. Kavanaughed looked down at her thoughtful.

"Prickly female, aren't you?"

She glared.

A dark smile curved his lips. "The evening isn't over yet, cub."

And it wasn't.

Annina awoke feeling used, abused, satiated. Thoroughly limber and relaxed. A glow suffused her, memories from the previous night clamoring to crowd out the mornings task. But she had a duty to her family. And it began with a clear head to negotiate her Boon.

Rising from Kavanaugh's rumpled bed, she entered the shower, taking her time to allow the hot stream to ease muscle aches and bruises. Annina swore. The male was… inventive. And athletic. A year of trying to keep up with him- her heart began to race. In anticipation or fear, she wasn't certain.

Now that her head was beginning to clear- she found she could think better with him absent. Annina began to reconsider what she knew about him. He'd made love to her like a male starving, then held her afterwards with the care of someone handling something precious. Not for the first time she wondered if he'd asked to be sent to this territory. And realized he must have known that upon arrival he'd be presented with a mandatory choice of a semi-permanent mate. Had he wanted a female of his own, maybe even a cub- was that one of the reasons why he'd chosen to come here? If it was, then it made her even more valuable than she'd previously supposed, and placed her in a much better bargaining position. Annina sighed, almost wishing they could just be. Her heart wasn't into using Bear for her Clan's gain.

"Your heart is pounding," Kavanaugh said from the door. She jumped, yelping.

He leaned against the lintel, arms folded across a bare chest, eyes glinting in amusement. "Sorry."

Bracing a hand on the tiled wall, Annina stared at him, lips pursed. Damn, he looked good. "Why don't you come in here and apologize?"

"So soon?" he murmured. "I would have thought you were… all worn out. I must not have treated you properly last night."

Annina snorted. Her pussy was raw, her thighs sore from a marathon of exercise. "If you had treated me anymore properly you would be at my funeral. Besides, it's the other way around. I'm supposed to worry about pleasing you."

His head tilted. She washed her body under his regard, stroking the puff along her skin with long, deliberate strokes.

"A sex slave is fun for a night- but for an entire year?" He shook his head. "Do you know, I was going to piss off the entire territory by not choosing last night?"

She froze, the water catching up to her ministrations and rinsing the lather down the drain. She shut off the nozzles and stepped out, grabbing a towel as she approached him.

"Why weren't you going to choose, Eldest?"

"Kavanaugh." His finger brushed her cheek. "Because I don't want a clan viper in my bed, ready to strike at a moment's notice. I want a lover, a… mate."

Annina didn't move. His words only confirmed her developing suspicions. A male who wanted a family would be more pliable- and more dangerous. "But you did choose."

"I did." His head dipped, mouth hovering over hers. She lifted her chin, just enough, and their lips brushed. He kissed her, slow and sensuous, then stepped back. "We have a Boon to talk about. Get dressed."

He'd said to get dressed, and she hadn't packed a bag so she shrugged, approaching a door she assumed had to be a closet and opened it. Chose a shirt at random. It was big enough, though a little tight around the chest- no matter since she simply left the top buttons undone. It covered her to mid thigh, which was good enough for modesty's sake- he'd already seen every inch of her anyway.

Following her nose, she found Kavanaugh in the kitchen. Cooking. Zeke looked up when she stopped.

"He won't burn it," he said, motioning her to a seat. Kavanaugh snorted, but didn't turn around. She pulled up a chair, running a hand through her hair, tugging uselessly at the shirt to get a bit more length out of it. Zeke's eyes roved over her appreciatively, a small smile curving his lips.

"Shouldn't I-"

Kavanaugh's growl shut her up. Zeke laughed. "Do me a favor, Fire Eagle. He hates subservient shit. Except in bed- from what I hear, and I heard plenty last night, so I will be getting some earplugs, thank you very much. So if he wants to cook, or fetch his own paper, or wipe his own ass- don't protest. So... about that job."

Kavanaugh turned, pointing a spatula towards him, lip curled in a snarl.

"Zeke!"

Annina looked at Zeke from the corner of her eye, who was balancing his chair on its hind legs, looking smug.

"How about a raise then, cuz?"

"You're related?" she asked, looking between them. They didn't look anything alike.

Kavanaugh looked aggrieved. "Yes. And he's on a five-year contract. I will consider any further attempts to poach an act of war."

She held up her hands. "Clan Fire Eagle yields."

He set a plate in front of her. Steak, lovingly seared and then left to rest in its juices. Fluffy eggs smothered in melting cheese. Biscuits heaped with butter and syrup. Annina moaned in pleasure, inhaling with her eyes closed.

"This is better than the sex," she said without thinking. Her lids flew open when she realized what she'd said.

Zeke slanted a look at Kavanaugh as she blushed.

Bear's mouth twisted sardonically as he sat with his own plate. "I'll take what I can get," he said. "I'm not a young man."

She fluttered her lashes at him. "You won't be getting the senior citizen discount any time soon, lover."

He regarded her a moment, then dug into his own plate. There were several moments of happy silence as they finished breakfast. She eyed the skillet on the stove.

"Eat up, you'll need your strength," Zeke said.

When she was settled back in her chair, Kavanaugh spoke. "Zeke is my witness. Do you want a representative here?"

She pushed aside her plate. Time for business. "No. A signed contract and your witness will do."

His eyes fixed on her. All trace of the lover was gone; only Bear remained.

"What Boon will clan Fire Eagle have of me for your year and a day submission?"

She inhaled. Placed her hands flat on the table in front of her. And told him. Told him about the fishing charters, her grandfather's mismanagement in his elder years. Told him how Blade wanted to usurp her clan's wealth when the charters came back up to the local council for ratification soon. Kavanaugh watched her, expression unsurprised. Annina was sure he already knew the disputes of the territory.

"What would you have me do, Annina?" he asked.

"I want your voice in the Council. I want to make sure the charters remain in my Clan. And I want to take over the business and financial management of my Clan."

Without his support, she was nearly certain the council would vote for Blade. And that would be a disaster, not only financially. Whatever bad blood was between her parents and Blade would erupt and Annina had no illusions that Terrence would use his newfound power to drive her family out of the territory- or even into a grave.

"A Boon, Annina, is usually more of the nature of a personal favor. There is a reason why it is not of a political nature."

She knew that. Knew that his support could be construed as favoritism, could get him into trouble with the North American council.

"I know," she whispered. "My mother- she wanted me to ask for a guard to protect me, but-"

"Why do you need a guard?" Zeke asked.

Annina fiddled with her fork. "There have been... a few incidents." She found she was reluctant to say more. Was reluctant to appear personally weak, or needy- or worse, hysterical.

"Have you been threatened?" Kavanaugh asked. She looked down at her plate. Bear rose, looking down at her. "Very well, but I want something in return, Annina, as what you are asking is a bit more complicated than a traditional Boon."

She waited.

He leaned down, placing a hand near hers, and took her lips in a kiss. When he pulled away, his eyes bored holes into hers.

Heart racing, she asked, "What would you have?"

"Don't go on birth control."

Her heart jumped. The one sentence told her everything she needed to know.

CHAPTER FOUR

Annina left the company of her Grandfather, frustration and anger seething inside her like a witch's brew ready to over boil. His words infuriated her- calm and measured, asking her if perhaps she was nothing more to The Bear than a convenient amenity of the territory. Good enough to warm his bed but not due the consideration of entertaining her requested Boon.

If Grandfather had known exactly what she had asked for, he probably would have added a few more choice words.

As it was, she drove her SUV into town where Kavanaugh kept an office- an actual office- where he would be at this time of day. Disconcerting at first, seeing how... businesslike he approached his management of the Territory. But after thinking about it, why not? A business, a small government- it was both those things, with Kavanaugh as its appointed King. A King whose consort was about to make the afternoon miserable if she didn't calm herself now.

Annina sat in the vehicle for several minutes slowing her breathing and attempting to wash away the insulting words seared into her mind. It would do her no good to offend a man whose ego and temper were still relatively unknown. Unfailingly kind and courteous during the last two weeks, scorching passionate at night, Annina found no fault in how he treated her- other than every time she asked about the Boon, he brushed her off.

"Are you coming in?"

Opening her eyes, realization dawned at just how vivid the images behind her lids were- she hadn't been aware she'd closed them.

Unbuckling the seatbelt, she slid out of the vehicle, leaving the keys in the ignition.

"Have you had lunch yet?" Zeke asked. "I was just about to go get sandwiches when you pulled up."

"No, thank you. I'm trying to cut back on my carbs."

He glanced at her, pale brow raised over icy gray eyes. A tiny furrow appeared between his brows. "What for?"

Annina snorted. Oh, to be a tall- well, *taller-* lean blond like Zeke, completely unaware of the struggles of being a curvy girl among a community of slender nymphettes. The fact that she was a shifter made it worse- the jokes growing up were relentless.

"You need to eat," he pressed. "You're a shifter. If you don't eat-"

She fluttered her hands in the air as he opened the front door. "Alright, alright. Veggie sub with cheese and extra mayo."

"Veggie."

She could tell by his tone what he thought about that. Turning, she glared at him until his thin lips quirked and he backed out the door in defeat.

"He isn't much of a salad man," Kavanaugh said behind her.

Annina turned, heart rate spiking as it always did after she'd been away from him for any length of time.

The Bear stood before her, calm almond eyes focused on her face. Light brown hair with a slight curl just brushed his shoulders- broad shoulders that led to hands she knew could be both gentle and rough, depending on whether he wanted to savor her or fuck her raw.

He closed the distance between them, placing a kiss on her forehead. "Did your meeting with Grandfather go well?"

It was a sign of respect that he said 'Grandfather' and not 'your Grandfather.' An acknowledgment of the Fire Eagle Clan head's status as an elder. One of the small courtesies that over the last two weeks had begun to endear Kavanaugh to her. A male with his power, reputation and political backing wasn't expected to be courteous, didn't have to be soft-spoken and gentle, almost humble in public. But he was, and it emphasized his strength all the more. Weak males never gave way.

"It went about the way you expected it would," she replied, then pressed her lips closed on her sharp tone.

He brushed her cheek with a knuckle. "I wasn't aware I had any expectations."

She tugged on one of her long braids, frustrated. "He wants to know why I haven't been granted a Boon as of yet," she said, pointedly. "I haven't told him what I asked for, so he isn't aware that it's more... complicated than usual."

Kavanaugh took a small step back, neutrality replacing some of the warmth in his eyes. She knew he didn't like discussing the Boon- she'd broken an unspoken tradition and instead of asking for money or some small piece of land, or fruit trees, or jewelry, she'd asked for him to intercede in the next Council meeting and ensure her family retained fishing rights over the Wenatchi River wild salmon when the charters came up for ratification. A political matter that as territory head, he should be non-partisan in adjudicating.

"Would you like me to speak with him so he is assured I'm not unhappy with you?"

She blushed. Did she want her consort to tell her Grandfather not to worry, the sex was just fine, and payment for services rendered would be forthcoming soon? Hell, no.

"I see." He looked at her, and for a moment Annina hated his measuring look. "It's no light thing you are asking, as you're aware. My answer still hasn't changed- I need time to determine what is best for the territory. If it is in everyone's best interest that Fire Eagle retains the charters, and the income, that is how my counsel will go." He paused, allowing silence to emphasize his words. "Now, are you hungry? Zeke will be back soon."

Annina knew it was fair- on the surface. To an outsider. Knew he didn't have her knowledge of the treachery of the Blade Clan, and the disaster that would fall on them all if Terrence Blade had control over that income- which supported several Clans in the territory, not just Fire Eagle.

She shook her head. "I'm not hungry yet. I have a few more errands to run and then I'll return."

Avoiding his eyes, Annina turned and left.

She took the one road out of town that led to the mountain lodge, the place the Welcoming and all other territory and official Clan business was conducted. Well, where most of the community business was conducted, period. Despite having built the town over a hundred years ago, the old ways died hard. She would sit inside and smoke some herb from her hidden stash and try to clear her mind, assess what was the best course of action. There were two men in her life being difficult, and she didn't understand why when all she wanted was for the people of the territory to be fed and sheltered- why couldn't Kavanaugh see that? And why was Grandfather so... critical of her when he knew she was trying her best?

At first, she thought her tire had blown. The sudden loud pop of rubber startled her. She swore, vehicle swerving as she got it under control and pulled over onto the side of the dirt road. When her windshield shattered, Annina knew it wasn't just a flat tire. She threw herself out of the door, acting on instinct, clothing splitting as her body raced through the change in record time. It was a skill of hers, one that proved the purity of her bloodline; her changes were accomplished in seconds rather than long, agonizing minutes.

She rose up on her hind legs, over six feet tall and several tons of furious black Bear, roaring a challenge. The tatters of her clothing hanging around her. Another bullet whizzed past, shattering tree bark behind her. Annina's head swung towards the direction of its travel and rather than running away, she ran towards it, crashing through the forest with a ferocity ignited by fury, unadulterated by fear.

But there were no more bullets and by the time she shifted back to human form and found where the shooter had abandoned an ideal perch from which to watch the road, she knew he or she was long gone.

Shoulder aching, she turned to walk back to her car. Lifted a hand almost absently as she glanced down at the shoulder and swore again, clasping her hand over the bleeding wound. A flesh wound, for sure, but now that she was aware of it, the pain blossomed with a vengeance. There was a set of spare clothing in the truck but no bandages.

Gritting her teeth, she dressed in the comfortably worn broomstick skirt and t-shirt, the kind of comfort clothing that could be worn in a store or to church in a pinch, and found the scraps of her former shirt in the road, shaking the cloth free of any loose dirt and using it to staunch the wound as best she could. She turned the SUV around and drove carefully back into town, wondering if this was enough to convince Kavanaugh that the Blades should never get their hands on the fishing charters.

Zeke tended to the wound while The Bear sat in his chair, still. She would have thought him unaffected but for the white of his knuckles and tension in his jaw. That, and the way Zeke kept glancing at him. When her flesh was properly cleaned and bandaged- though she wondered why he even bothered, it healed even as he tended to it- Zeke stood up from his crouch.

"See, all better now," he said soothingly, a hair away from fussy. "Just a little scratch, I bet it *doesn't even hurt.*"

She looked at him askance. "Of course it-"

His gaze flicked again towards Kavanaugh and Annina suddenly felt the tension in the room, thick like a blanket of the Elder's happy dream weed. Kavanaugh's stillness, Zeke nervousness.

"Can you take me to where you were shot?" Kavanaugh asked, rising, voice perfectly casual.

Annina hesitated. She wasn't a fool. "Are you alright?"

He smiled, grim. "Despite the impression Zeke's vapors have given you, I'm not about to lose control anytime soon, my dear." But his gaze touched on her wound and then danced away, mouth twisting before smoothing back to neutrality.

She shrugged, pulling her hair over the uninjured shoulder. Too bad Zeke didn't have a brush handy to get the twigs out. "Yes. It's the road I usually travel along to get to the lodge."

Kavanaugh gestured to the door, opening it so she could precede him. "Did anyone know you were going there today?"

She frowned, touching his chest as she passed. The muscle flexed under the brush of her fingers. "I didn't tell anyone. But I visit there several times a week, sometimes to meet with family, sometimes just to... think. Anyone could camp out for a few hours a day and probably stumble on me eventually."

"I'm going to nose around," Zeke said as they left the building. Kavanaugh locked it behind them, nodding his head at his guard.

"Come on," The Bear said. "Let's see if there is anything to be found."

Kav was an SUV kind of man. Zeke preferred the intimacy, the power of a bike beneath his legs. The wind in his hair and the bugs between his teeth on a warm summer day. Liked the way the roar of the engine announced him before he arrived. He felt at one with the bike, as if it were an extension of his beast, yowling angrily to be released.

To be allowed to hunt.

"Not today," he whispered.

He roared down the two-lane main street through town, not caring that the noise of his bike was incongruous in the sleepy forest quiet. If the Blade really was behind the attempt on Ann's life, the Blade would die.

Because Zeke was Zeke, he already knew where to find the male. The first thing he'd done when arriving in town- two weeks before the

Welcoming and anyone even knew he was around- was to stalk and pin down the movements of all the Clan Elders. He wasn't the kind of male who liked to stop and ask for directions, especially if there was an enemy at his back.

When he pulled up to a two-story frame house with wraparound porch, the Blade looked up, unsurprised. Children played in the yard in a wide circle around a smoking barbecue pit. Adults surrounded the pit, males with braided hair and females in long skirts. Zeke parked and dismounted, strolling towards Terrence with a studied casualness. Before the Clan Elder met him half way, Zeke already knew the locations of every adult shifter in the yard and had a pin on several he'd seen moving through the wide front windows.

"Enforcer," Terrence greeted him around an old-fashioned pipe. His dark eyes were narrow, graying braid draped over one shoulder and woven with strands of beads and strips of colored leather. From what Zeke understood, the decorations announced to those who knew, the Clan and rank of the person in front of him.

"Blade."

"Welcome to the fire. Can I get you a beer?"

"I didn't come to socialize."

The Elder snorted. "I didn't think you did, pale face. But as you get older, you tend to learn the value of civility in dealing with an enemy. Try to survive long enough to learn, boy."

Zeke watched him with the stillness of a raptor eyeing lunch. "Are you an enemy, Blade?"

Terrence puffed a ball of fragrant air into his face, grinned cannily. "I wouldn't think so. But I figure that'll be up to you- and The Bear unless he's already enamored of that stubborn bitch in his bed."

A rumble slipped from Zeke's chest. He knew, even after only two weeks, that the girl was stubborn. And single-minded and hot tempered. But he also suspected she was loyal to a fault and fierce in defense of her loved ones. He liked her.

"Down, boy. No need for violence here. I'm going back to the fire. You have business with me, you can come sit and have a beer. And when the meat is ready, you can have some of that, too."

The old Bear turned his back on Zeke and walked away. He followed- because he wanted to, that's why, and soon found himself squeezed between a middle-aged woman with a toddler on her lap and a lanky young man old enough to *sit* with the grownups but too young to be allowed to *speak* in public among the grownups. Zeke felt... uncomfortable. How was he supposed to threaten and growl around females and children?

Someone shoved a beer in his hand and after he'd popped the tab and taken a swig, Terrence looked his way again.

"Now, what brings you out here with that look on your face?" He waved around the circle. "Speak freely, these are all my family."

What the hell. "There was an attempt on Annina's life today."

Blade cracked a laugh. The female next to Zeke snorted, while the youth listened with unabashed interest. "And you want to know if I had something to do with it. Stupid. I don't need to kill that girl." He grinned again, and this time it was edged with malice. "She needs a lesson in respect for her Elders, but I've no need to kill the cub."

"You want the fishing charters."

Terrence puffed, eyes squinting up at the afternoon sun. His brown skin was smooth, age showing only in the thin lines at the corner of his eyes.

"And I'm going to get them. Again, I don't need to kill her."

Zeke understood. The male's posture, his tone of voice, the calm of his expression- Blade believed with absolute certainty that he was going to be granted the fishing charters when they came up for ratification. Certainty like that only came from knowledge- knowledge held close to the chest to be presented at the most opportune time.

Zeke finished the beer and stood. "I'll let Kavanaugh know."

Blade stared up at him impassively. At Zeke's feet, the toddler poked his boots, leaning over in an attempt the chew the scuffed leather. The female holding...it...pulled it away slightly and it yowled, upset. A toy was shoved between its budding teeth and it quieted, though grumpily. Zeke shuffled away... just a little.

"You'll let him know what, boy?"

"That you didn't try to kill his mate."

CHAPTER FIVE

Zeke pulled off the side of the road a few miles away and spoke briefly to Kav. What his cousin decided to do with Zeke's opinion was up to him. Traveling along the road, Zeke decided to do a little more exploring of the countryside, choosing a side road at random. The path through the forest was tamped down by the use of SUV's and plenty of feet both bear and human, but other than that no one had bothered to lay gravel. So when the forest opened up to a rough circle of cleared land all of a sudden, he slowed to investigate.

A clear, glass-walled building sat at the back of the clearing, almost at the forest's edge, with rows of neatly turned dirt in front of it, full of plants in various stages of growth. Zeke turned off the bike and swung down, a sudden descending silence warning him that his approach hadn't gone unnoticed. Even the crickets were quiet. As he came closer, he realized the building was a greenhouse and could see the plants inside- and a storage shed sitting partially in the shade of trees.

"Hello?" he called, eyeing the shed. Hoping whoever was in there didn't come out with a rifle. Around here he wouldn't be surprised at that sort of thing. People were friendly enough- but wary of strangers.

The shed door opened abruptly and a woman stepped out. He grinned, momentarily diverted that his first mind was correct- she was holding a rifle, albeit butt down in the dirt. But holding it as if she knew how to swing it up, point and shoot faster than he would be able to get it away from her. The next thing he noticed was she was beautiful.

It hit him in the gut. He wasn't normally a male turned by a pretty face- and if he really analyzed it, her face was no prettier than several others he'd seen- but there was something about her. Something about the lithe body, and shining fall of dark hair covering her

68

shoulders, framing an olive brown face with full lips and wide, opal eyes.

"I know who you are," she said, voice soft and firm. "What do you want?"

He took a minute to reply. "I was... exploring the area. I saw the greenhouse and was curious."

"Curious." She tilted her head, blinking long lashes. "You don't look like a vegetarian to me. Or a gardener."

"I eat vegetables." He paused. Made himself tell the truth. "When Kav makes me."

"Kav?" Her eyes widened. "The Bear. The Bear makes you eat your vegetables?"

He eyed her, curious and oddly hungry at the way her lips pressed together. Zeke felt the urge to explain himself- he didn't want her to think he was a wuss, or anything.

"Well, he doesn't really make me. He just won't make any of the good stuff unless I eat the healthy stuff, too." Zeke paused, considering. "Though he hasn't been cooking much lately."

"I'll bet he hasn't." She shook her head, reaching in the shed to set the rifle down. "Well, if you're curious, I'll give you a tour. I don't get many visitors up here." She trailed off, and he could see the thoughts rolling across her face as she paused.

"I'm harmless, girl."

"Hmm. That's what the dangerous ones always say."

They drove out to the site where Annina had first heard the shots. Because of the shape of the mountains in the background peeking through trees, and her lifetime of familiarity, she was able to tell Kavanaugh when to pull over. Splintered tree bark confirmed her recollection and they spent several minutes determining where a shooter would have hidden, waiting. Discussing who would have known to wait for her at that particular spot, at that particular time.

Kavanaugh's cell rang and not for the first time Annina wished she had the ears of a wolf. Kavanaugh listened to his cousin speak for several minutes, responses non-committal, his eyes on her the entire time. Dark, inscrutable, even as the early evening breeze teased his curls.

"What did he say?" Annina asked when her lover disconnected. He seemed to consider his words.

"He doesn't think Blade had anything to do with it."

"What?" She was stunned. Betrayal welled up in her chest, a hard lump that temporarily stole her words.

"Annina, I trust Zeke's judgment. He has yet to fail me. He spoke to the man, and Blade said he didn't try to kill you- has no reason to do so."

"He has every reason!" Was Zeke blind as well as deaf? "Why would Zeke fall for his deceit?"

"Annina, have you ever considered any other possibility?"

"Have I considered that there is someone running around the territory who wants the fishing charters and doesn't want me to be successful in garnering the territory council vote- someone who has yet to make themselves known?"

"Exactly."

His stoic calm infuriated her. He didn't respond to her sarcasm; not even with the flick of an eyelash did he betray ire at her tone, or rise to further defend his cousin.

"No, I haven't considered."

"Perhaps it's time you did." The words fell between them with the finality of a command. They stared at each other, dark eyes hot and cold, a silent battle of wills.

Kavanaugh sighed, closed the small distance between them. Her hands rose automatically, not to hit home, though she was frustrated enough, but to tangle in the cloth of his shirt. Large hands wrapped around hers, warm with a solid strength, trapping her against him. He lowered his head, slowly enough that she could pull away if she wished, but Annina wasn't quite foolish enough to deny him. Didn't want to deny him. His lips brushed her own, soft and seeking. When she opened beneath him, his tongue slipped into her mouth, playing and suckling as his teeth nibbled. He pulled her closer so her soft body was flush against the hard planes of his.

"Patience, little bear," he said against her mouth. "You're fierce in defense of your loved ones. But learn to temper your love with wisdom. It will keep you from learning a lesson the hard way."

She tore away from him, aware that after a moment, he allowed it. And saw, for a split second, a flare of heat in his eyes. Felt a petty satisfaction that The Bear didn't like his femalepulling away, retreating. Denying him.

"Don't forget what you promised me," Kavanaugh said.

Annina took a deep breath, calming her temper. "I-"

The ringing of her cell interrupted her. She pulled it out of her jean pocket, pressed connect.

"Yes?"

"Come to the greenhouse," Halcione demanded, excited tones telling Annina this was something more than a regular social call. Her cousin was rarely demanding.

"What's wrong?"

"Nothing's wrong. Just come, and hurry up."

Annina stared at the cell then shrugged. "Do you mind dropping me off at my cousin's? I'll make my way back."

He glanced around, nodding. "There's nothing to learn here. Let's go."

Kavanaugh was reluctant to allow her out of his sight, but Annina assured him she was safe enough with Halcione. The attempts over the last few weeks always came when she was alone. And if she were honest with herself, a seed of doubt had wriggled into her mind. What if they were nothing more than malicious pranks designed to irritate her? After all, if someone- Blade- really wanted her dead, shouldn't she be dead by now?

Halcione was inside the greenhouse, bent over the rows of herbs growing in a... fragrant... array. Annina hadn't been here in a while, preferring to deal with her own small kitchen gardens and respecting that this was her cousin's personal space.

"What's going on?" Annina asked when the younger female looked up.

Halcione's night black eyes sparkled, a small smile curving her lips. She'd pulled her hair back in a loose braid to keep it out of the way.

"I met the enforcer."

Annina blinked. It wasn't what she'd expected to hear. "Okaaaay. You could have told me that over the phone."

Halcione waved a hand. "That's incidental- though interesting. No, what I wanted to tell you- Grandfather."

Annina turned. Grandfather walked through the door and Halcione rose, walking towards him to plant a kiss on his cheek. Tall, his white braids fell in rivulets over spare shoulders, blue and orange beads of their Clan tinkling at the tips. Annina tensed, still smarting from his earlier words.

"Well, girl? You called. I'm here."

Annina frowned, now doubly curious. If Halcione had called both her and Grandfather, it meant it was Clan business and not something personal.

"I wanted to show you this," she said, caressing the tiny leaf of an herb with the tips of her fingers. "This is the way to solve the fishing charter problem."

"I don't see what herbs-"

"Powerful herbs," Halcione interrupted Grandfather. "Herb's that a major pharmaceutical company is willing to pay money for."

"Halcione." Annina sighed. "You aren't making sense."

"About a year ago a representative came nosing around- I caught him in the woods. Well, it was a team really. There were foraging for a rare plant they knew was in the area. They use it to make a medicine."

"What kind of medicine, Granddaughter?"

Halcione shrugged. Annina knelt next to her, bending over to inhale the scent of the plant. After a moment, it made her slightly dizzy.

"Don't do that," her cousin said. "Anyway, the reps wanted to pay us locals-" Halcione's mouth twisted "-to gather the plant for them. I told him I could do one better, I could cultivate a strain so they had a guaranteed supply. I've been spending my time learning how to grow it."

Annina wasn't convinced. "Can they get it anywhere else?"

Halcione shook her head. "No, it only grows in this region. And not at all in the colder months. Nina, they are willing to pay big bucks. I've got documents and everything."

Annina rocked back on her heels, mind swirling. "Halcione, of course this is a good thing, but I still don't see what it has to do with the fishing charters."

Halcione looked down, starring hard at the rows of plants. "Don't you think it's time we gave them up? Our family has monopolized them for generations now."

Annina stared at her, aghast. "What are you talking about, Hal? We need that income."

"With this herb, we can replace that income. And because no one knows about it- I have an exclusivity agreement- then there won't be any fights." She looked at Grandfather. "Dada, don't you see this would be a good thing? How many times have our families almost come to blows over the charters? All the politics- everyone is tense and unhappy. We're losing control."

"Don't worry about control of the territory, Granddaughter," Grandfather said, words distinct. "I will never give that up- no matter what difficulties stand in the way."

They discussed the development a while longer, before Grandfather cut the meeting off with a declaration that nothing would be rushed into.

"I will see your cousin to her home," Grandfather said to Halcione. Annina didn't protest. They might have their differences, but he was still Elder.

On the drive deeper into the forest where Kavanaugh kept his 'cabin', the silence was a tense one. After he'd pulled up, Annina fumbled with her belt. His hand on her wrist stopped her.

"My words this morning were harsh, Annina. You are my true heir, and you have done your duty to the Clan diligently."

Annina's anger softened, some of the ignoring hurt dissipating. It was an apology, one as frank as she could expect from a man with Grandfather's dignity. She leaned over and kissed his cheek.

"Your wisdom is always welcome in my ears, Grandfather."

Kavanaugh wasn't yet home, though it was almost dark. Annina set to making a meal, a routine she'd carried over from living on her own. Though The Bear, apparently, cooked- it made her uncomfortable to allow him to do so. Except for maybe breakfast in bed the morning after a particularly hearty bout of love play. But as a woman and a daughter, she was far more comfortable serving him than the other way around. It was just how she'd been raised.

When he came home, she had fowl and fish on the table with an assortment of vegetables and homemade rolls.

"I could get used to this," he said, sliding an arm around her waist and kissing her thoroughly.

His lips warmed her, the firmness of his hands on her waist. He handled her as if she was dainty, a scrap of lace in the wind.

"I'm hungry," he said against her mouth, the growl in his tone letting Annina know he wasn't referring to food.

"There's plenty of fish."

He paused, a rubber band silence stretching between them for a moment. "You're like a burr caught in fur."

Hoisting her up, he backed her up against the nearest wall. Wrapping her legs around his waist, she ground her mound into the hardening bulge at his crotch.

"You can always toss me back in the river, Eldest," she replied, coolly, even as her body clamored to be taken. "There are plenty of little, pretty fish to bait you."

For the second time that day, his infuriatingly cool dark eyes flared, hinting at a hotter forge underneath the icy calm. "And you're the hook that would gut me if I dared."

"I would never, Eldest." She lowered her lashes, baring teeth at him in a smile. "I understand politics. I'm a big girl."

His hand rose to cup her heavy breast, pinching the nipple with a deliberate pressure that sent shoots of fire into her clit when she gasped from the brief pain.

"Yes, you are, aren't you? A big girl with a will to match her body... too much for a weak man to handle." He lowered his mouth to her neck, sharp edges of his teeth grazing her skin. "I am not a weak male, Annina Fire Eagle."

Her hand slid in between their bodies, reaching for the button and zipper of his jeans to free his cock. Rapping her hand around it, she squeezed, giggling when he hissed.

"Are you laughing at me?"

He returned the favor, pulling up the gauzy fabric of her broomstick skirt to bunch around her waist, ruthless as he delved into her core.

"Wet." The dark satisfaction in his tone sent a shiver up her spine. His fingers plunged into her and she moaned. "Who is laughing now?"

He was clever. He fucked her with his fingers as his thumb rubbed against her clit, turning her into a mewling mess of a woman with fish the furthest thing from her mind.

"You belong to me, Annina. Not Fire Eagle. My interests are yours."

A little sanity returned. Was he trying to manipulate her? Control her with sex?

"My family-"

"What did you promise me?" he snarled.

For a moment, her heart beat with fear rather than excitement. His pupils enlarged, almost eclipsing the irises, lips drawn back over lengthening incisors.

"Don't make me betray my family," she whispered, throat dry.

His fingers withdrew from her slick pussy, his cock taking their place. She cried out when he sheathed himself in one hard thrust, her head jerking against the wall with the force of his penetration.

"What. About. Me?"

Each word was truncated by a breath stealing thrust. He fucked her with a furor that left no room for words, barely room for anger. Her fear only added spice to her arousal-Kavanaugh was right. He was not a weak male, and it only made him more dangerous to her. To her heart. Because she was not a weak female, and inside she yearned for a Bear to match her.

"Mine," he said, free hand tangling in her hair at the nape. He jerked her head to the side, giving his teeth access to the flesh between her throat and collarbone. "Say it."

"Yours." The word trembled on her lips.

Teeth sank into her flesh, the searing pain eclipsed by the sudden, nearly overwhelming tangle of foreign thought and emotion in her mind as their bond snapped into place. Strand by strand, Kavanaugh had allowed it to form on its own over the last few weeks. Now, from whatever perverse masculine possessiveness that spurred him, he forced the remaining strand into being, claiming her with the thrust of his cock and snap of his teeth. Annina screamed as her orgasm overtook her, leaving her body like so much jelly, boneless and without form. He followed her a moment later, roaring his release as hot seed filled her pussy, their cum intermingling.

He braced against the wall as her legs loosened their vise like grip, sliding to the floor. For a moment, she thought her knees wouldn't hold her, but forced herself to remain standing. She licked her lips, struggling for breath.

"What have you done?" she whispered. "Kavanaugh, this can't be undone."

Slowly, he stepped back, his public mask of calm snapping back into place. But they were fully mated now and despite his internal barriers, she sensed his turmoil.

"I said you were mine," he replied, icy. "I don't waste my words."

CHAPTER SIX

She cleaned herself up, and then made her way back into the dining room.

"I'm hungry," her mate growled, ceasing his pacing as she entered.

She smiled as he eyed the dishes. "Wash your hands."

He slanted a glance at her as he complied, more thoroughly than she had right to expect from a male. "Mama Bear," he said, amused.

"Where is Zeke?"

"He'll be along."

"I'll fix him a plate."

After putting the enforcer's plate in the oven to stay warm, Annina took her seat.

"Does your cousin need something?"

Annina paused, fork in the air. "And if she did?"

He blinked slowly, tearing a piece of bread and slathering it with butter, all while looking at her. "Your family is important, Annina. Just because I can't guarantee you the outcome you want regarding the charters doesn't mean I won't see to their welfare." He paused. "I know you are your Grandfather's Heir and second, in all but name."

True. Her father had no interest in leading, preferred fishing and perfecting his leatherwork skills.

Annina considered what she would reveal. "Halcione has happened upon another revenue source- one that is replenishable, that we can keep quiet to avoid competition. She wants me to consider focusing on that rather than the fishing."

"She sounds wise. Monoculture is dangerous, little bear. One bad season and your entire crop is gone."

She considered him, annoyed- and even more annoyed because she knew he was right.

"Fish are not crops," she replied, tearing bits of chicken into tiny, uniform pieces.

Her pussy throbbed, the mark in her neck where he had bit her also making itself known. She saw him glance at it, as if aware of her discomfort. Unrepentant.

"And stubborn children are not fishermen," he retorted.

Her fork clattered on her plate. "If wanting what is best for my family and my territory makes me a stubborn child," she said through gritted teeth. "Then so be it. You mated this stubborn child. Without asking."

He lifted a brown, arrogance in the line of his shoulders. "I don't have to ask. I take."

She surged to her feet, temper unleashed. "Take your cock between your hand tonight," she hissed. "You won't be taking me."

Annina ran into Zeke on the way out. Or rather, he planted himself in her way.

"I heard the argument," he said.

"Stop eavesdropping then."

He frowned. "You're placing him in a bad position. Please his mate, or do what's right.

"Why doesn't anyone see that what is right is what I want?" She wanted to tug her hair out in frustration. "My family has been caretaker of these waters for generations. We have made the people wealthy, kept the land balanced. My Grandfather needs to step down, for certain, but I am capable of fixing the mistakes he's made in the last few years."

"Annina." Zeke's voice gentled. "You can't follow the right path if you are staring into the sun."

"Don't try and use my own family's proverbs against me," she snapped. "Why don't you go eat and leave me alone for now, okay?"

He stepped out of her way, silence ominous. She hurried out, slamming the door behind her.

She didn't return to his cabin that night, instead going to her small abandoned house, refusing to admit to herself that she was trying to teach Kavanaugh a lesson. But the night was miserable. In the short time they'd been together, she'd become used to his warmth at her side, the rumble of his breathing deep in the night and waking up to his cock sheathed deep inside of her body, responding to him even in sleep.

So she was awake when early the next morning her cell rang. She considered not answering, but didn't want to push her childishness. She regretted her temper- mostly she always did, after she had time to cool down. Intending to apologize, Annina answered the phone softly.

"Good morning."

"I've called a Circle at dawn," The Bear said, brusquely, then hung up.

She put the cell down. Then got up and moved.

Annina wore the traditional dress of her people, heavily embroidered, her hair a straight fall of silk down her back. Grandfather sat cross-legged at her side, braids and beaded in orange and teal. The ceremonial heirloom vest of her family lovingly embroidered with stories from each generation worn over a linen, collarless shirt. Terrence Blade sat opposite of them, The Bear standing in the middle of the circle, naked but for a pair of jeans. Ready to shift at a moment's notice. There hadn't been a death at a circle in generations, so Annina didn't know if he was bare for show... or if he knew something she didn't know.

Kavanaugh watched the sky, waiting for the exact moment when the sun crested the mountains before lowering his head, dark eyes glittering.

"Elders," he said. "We are gathered to hear and judge a dispute over fishing rights to the Wenatchi River. Rights granted to the Council to assign as they see fit. Until now, they have seen fit to grant those rights to Clan Fire Eagle to oversee. They have done a fair job, but certain issues have arisen in the past several years. Blade states that Fire Eagle is no longer fit to manage the wealth of the people, and wants to be named overseer. Blade states it has evidence of wrongdoing and incompetence on the side of Fire Eagle."

Annina gasped, not able to believe her ears, or the betrayal. How could he? Kavanaugh ignored her, turning his body slightly towards Blade, who rose. Her eyes dropped to the yellow packet in his hand.

"What trickery is this?" Grandfather asked, the barest hint of a growl in his tone.

"Elders," Blade said, ignoring him. "I have had a spy in the Fire Eagle offices these past several months. The information I am about to present to you is factual, and gathered painstaking with attention to fairness over a period of time." He paused, turned to face Grandfather fully. Lifted an arm and pointed. "Shiloh Fire Eagle has been embezzling Wenatchi salmon profits and investing into private land held in trust for his own family- land he never intended be used by all the Clans for hunting and gathering. He has betrayed our trust, and I have the proof."

Terrence tossed the packet at Annina, who caught it squarely in her chest even as she surged to her feet, outraged.

Kavanaugh looked at her then, expression hard. "Sit down," he said softly.

"What is this bullshit?" she asked, glaring at Kavanaugh while holding the packet.

"Your Grandfather is mad," Terrence told her. "I haven't tried to kill you, girl. You need to look to the smoke in your lodge hiding under a blanket."

"Proof," Terrence replied. She glanced at him and for a moment saw pity in his face. But then it was gone, subsumed by his usual ironic implacability. "And if you're as stupid as he is, which I suspect you may be, you'll ignore it. But if you want to be the strongest Elder your Clan has seen in generations, you'll verify those documents, girl, and get your shit together."

Several other Clan heads began to speak up at once, a rare occurrence. The breach of civility added to the many shocks of the day.

Terrence held up a hand. "I'm not saying anything else. Fire Eagle has a right to answer those documents before I let the rest of you get your greedy claws on them."

"Annina." Kavanaugh said her name, quietly.

"Did you know about this?" she asked.

"What do you think?"

She turned and walked away, refusing to look at Grandfather, refusing to look at anyone. Several yards into the forest, she heard light footsteps following her.

"Nina!"

Annina paused, and only because it was Halcione calling her, who didn't deserve discourtesy.

"Do you think it's true?"

Halcione looked at her, doe eyes grave. "What's interesting is The Bear thinks it's true," she replied softly. "He didn't warn you."

Annina didn't move, expression stony. She trusted Kav, or she thought she had. It didn't reconcile, to suddenly not accept his judgement because she didn't like it. But she'd been a granddaughter far longer than she'd been a lover, or a mate.

Halcione was silent for several moments. "What are we going to do?"

"We?"

"We."

Sighing, she took a step back to lean on a tree, suddenly tired. "I'm going to review these documents, and then I'm going to figure out who the spy is."

"What if his accusations are true?"

"I don't know, Halcione. I don't have answers. I know that Grandfather isn't qualified to be over the Clan's business matters anymore. I know that if he's guilty of what Blade says he is..." she couldn't finish the statement. "Halcione, have I been wrong this entire time?"

"I don't know. But I know that if we've been wrong, we can fix it. Annina, Blade wouldn't have given you these papers if he didn't want to give you a chance. You heard what he said- you could be the strongest leader in several generations. I didn't even think he liked you. Or females, really."

Annina stared down at the packet in her hands. "He doesn't. I'm probably just not a real female to him. Too old and fat." She looked up at her cousin. "Go back to Grandfather. I need to be alone and think."

Think about what she'd been refusing to allow herself to consider. What Kavanaugh had been trying to tell her all along- that maybe what she thought she knew wasn't entirely correct.

Anger boiled in her blood. Convinced he'd withheld information from her, Annina wanted to charge back into the circle and call him out in front of every Clan head in the territory. She wanted to humiliate him beyond humiliation. She wanted to shift and use claws and teeth to strip flesh from bones. And she wanted to cry.

Annina slid down the tree, crossing her legs and opening the little metal tab keeping the envelop secure. She pulled out a sheaf of papers, began sorting through them one by one, throat dry. Eyes unblinking. There was too much to go through, but she recognized the small, neat handwriting of the least senior junior accountant in the office in town- the one who liked to make handwritten notes in the margins of all her reports. A small, precise human woman with such an absence of humor Annina had taken to avoiding her for fear of accidently offending the woman with a ribald joke or comment.

The sense of betrayal was strong. She felt the forest closing in on her and realized the documents in her hand were blurring.

She heard the steps approaching, just loud enough to give her warning. Her mate could have made his approach unknown if he'd wished. Kavanaugh knelt in the earth next to her, hands on the tops of his thighs.

"I haven't seen the documents," he said. "Is it bad?"

She looked up. "You already know what's here."

"Some. Not all. Blade wouldn't share everything he knew- he was certain I would tell you."

"Would you have?"

"Would you have believed me?"

"I still don't believe you. Or this."

His regard was steady. "Are you being willfully blind, little bear?"

"No." She rose to her feet, looked down at him. There was some regret in his expression. But not nearly enough. "I'm going to verify all the information here, and then I'll decide what to do."

"But is it enough for you to consider you may be wrong- about Blade, about your Grandfather, about the future of your Clan?"

Why was he pressing this? Did he want her Clan to fail?

He must have seen the frustration on her face. "You are strong enough to bear this, Annina."

The Bear rose, hand cupping the back of her neck as he pulled her towards him to capture her lips in a kiss. And not a comforting kiss, but one full of unspoken promise, and demand. Her free hand rose and tangled in his curls. She pressed against him, desperately seeking comfort. A moments respite from the unspoken weight of the entire Clan on her shoulders.

Or more than a moment.

Annina dropped the papers and deliberately collapsed her knees, pulling Kavanaugh down with her.

His brow shot up. "Here? Now?"

"Are you a prude?" she asked, a taunt in her voice. He bared teeth at her in a mock snarl.

"Some days you almost push me too far, female. The day you do... I hope you can handle the beast."

She knew he was at least half serious, so she didn't giggle. But it was a damn near thing. But when he grabbed her around the waist and flipped her over onto her knees, she didn't feel like laughing any more.

"No foreplay- just my cock in your pussy." He pulled her dress up over her ass, slapping a plump cheek with enough force to sting. She gasped, back arching. "Is that what you want?"

"Yes, please, Kavanaugh, I need this."

He caressed her stinging flesh, bending over her so his mouth was pressed against her ear, deep voice rumbling through her and bringing shivers to the surface of her skin. "I know you do. You'll get all you can take and more."

The sound of a zipper. He pushed her thighs apart, the head of his cock pressing against her entrance. Annina knew she was wet, felt the needy throb between her legs as she bucked against him, demanding his entrance. An evening breeze caressed her skin, the rustle of wind through trees and the song of crickets in her ear. She inhaled the scent of salty sweet pre cum beading on the tip of his cock, the heat of her arousal as he pressed into her with taunting slowness. Filling her, forcing himself in with punishing relentlessness, not giving her walls time to adjust to his mammoth width.

She stifled a gasp, head hanging down and widened her thighs, trying to somehow give him more room. She felt invaded, taken over, possessed. Helpless beneath him as he pulled out and then slid back in, pace increasing, hands grabbing her waist and pulling her ass flush against him so his cock ground inside of her pussy. Her silence broke, mewls of painful please tumbling from her throat.

"I didn't betray you," he said, fucking her in long, hard strokes. Tone as merciless as his cock. "I know what you think. But I've seen people like you before."

Annina tried to pull away from him, anger roused. He held her fast, a growl rumbling in his chest.

"People like me?" She gasped, nails lengthening and digging into the dirt. She twisted to look over her shoulder, snarling at him. "Let me go!"

He grinned at her, savage, eyes glowing in the dark. "Mine. Not letting go. Just take it. Enjoy me fucking you- you're mine to claim whenever I wish. However I wish. And people like you have to learn the hard way. They only believe what their own senses tell them. It's a strength- and a fatal flaw." He leaned over her, whispered in her ear. "Little Alpha."

Claws burst from her nails as she growled at him, her anger and desire roiling in a potent cocktail of heat and emotion. Thighs tensing, she gathered her strength in a single burst and flung herself away from him.

"Little Alpha?"

He rose to his full height, stalking her, cock hard and glistening, a life in his face she'd never seen before as if he delighted in her defiance, savored her anger... anticipated a challenge.

"You're young," he said, the timbre of his voice deepening. His Bear moved under the skin, shoulders widening, hair lengthening. Eyes tracking her with the bright intensity of a hunter. "You think everyone you love is good." He took a few more gliding steps towards her. She tensed even as her breasts tightened, body clamoring at her to go to him. "You can't conceive of a world where your love is rewarded with betrayal, where the people who raised you turn out to be idols made of crumbling clay."

"My Grandfather is not a traitor!" She rose to her feet, the cry wrenched from her throat, a howl of desperate denial- and leaped, barreling into his chest with a force he absorbed, wrapping strong arms around her and taking them both to the hard ground. But this time he covered her body from above, trapping her on her back as she snarled at him, her wrists slammed above her head and pinned in place.

"I don't give a flying fuck about your Grandfather," he said. "You are mine- not he." He cupped her mound with his free hand. "This is my reward for coming to this Territory- and I won't be cheated of it by your naiveté or his treachery. My mate- and in time, my cub."

And he yanked her dress back up for the second time that night, following the movement by pushing her legs apart with his knees and entering her in one thrust. She pulled back her knees, wrapping legs around his waist to give him full access, helpless to deny herself any longer. The tone of his voice when he claimed her, speaking of a child with a yearning that softened her heart- she couldn't remain angry. Not at him. He hadn't caused any of this mess, he was just the one sent to clean it up.

Annina's climax overtook her and for several moments thought, emotion and even vision vanished. There was only sensation, only the distant sound of his release and the feeling of seed inside her. Her pussy clenching and throbbing, the exultation of her body- which apparently had more sense than her stubborn mind.

When she tumbled back into reality she realized her hands were free, and promptly swung at him. He caught the swing, laughing and rolling onto his back so she draped across his body.

"Ah, little bear, you delight me."

He kissed her, hands roving up and down her back with a familiar affection. Pulling away, his lips brushed against her cheek.

"Take Zeke with you. No- no arguments. I would feel more... secure."

Annina stared at him. "What do you think is going to happen?"

"Annina, if Blade hasn't been trying to hurt you, who has? And what may it have to do with this evidence he's uncovered?"

"I'll take him."

CHAPTER SEVEN

Zeke humored them both. He allowed her to spend a total sum of ninety minutes in the office before shutting it down.

"It's late- go home, shag your mate, get some dinner. The morning is soon enough for this."

So they left, Annina dragging her feet because she knew she wouldn't be able to sleep that night. Adrenaline rushed through her veins like a turbo shot of espresso. In bed, she tossed and turned until Kavanaugh growled at her and tossed an arm and leg over her body to hold her still. Her body finally sent her to sleep from sheer exhaustion, but as soon as light peeked through the blinds, she was pushing out of bed and rushing through her routine in order to get back into town.

"Damn, female," Zeke growled. "Let me have at least one cup of coffee."

She whirled around, quickly searched through cabinets and brought out a travel mug, thunking it on the table next to him.

"Here."

He growled, but poured the coffee into the mug, muttering under his breath.

"Why are you so tired anyway?" she asked, eyes keen. "Where were you all night?"

The disadvantage of such pale skin made itself known when his cheeks turned... pink.

"Let's go," he said, pushing past her- rather hurriedly.

Annina smiled, filing the incident away to probe later when she was feeling more playful and less like she was strapped to a train track watching a locomotive approach.

Most of the main businesses were in town, except for people who worked from home, and the Fire Eagle Clan offices were no different.

They sported two accountants- one now, and she hoped she had the opportunity to fire the woman in person- a sales rep and an office manager. Annina kept her fingers in every pie, preferring the ambiguous role of 'owner' which gave her the freedom to do whatever task she wished. But mostly to make sure everyone else was doing their job to her satisfaction.

"Where's the new accountant?" she asked with a growl when she and Zeke entered the office.

The manager looked up from her desk near the back, curious. "Funny. I was just emailed a resignation. Something going on?"

That was one of the benefits of hiring an outsider. Utter neutrality when it came to Clan business. "Gather everyone in my office for a meeting. Ten minutes."

After the employees were gathered, Annina explained the situation. She was frank- if she was going to tear apart the business and pull out its insides, everyone needed to know what was happening. She set the accountants to pouring over financial records, the office manager to verifying independent contractor's payments and information. Any hole that involved a possible avenue to funnel money,

Annina wanted plugged. An exhausting three days later, she had the grim framework of a jagged puzzle.

Enough to confront her grandfather. Her suspiciousy silent on the subject grandfather.

"Let me do this alone," she asked Zeke quietly when they pulled up outside Grandfather's cabin. He chose to live in the woods, surrounded by forest and as far from modern intrusion as possible, and still have plumbing.

"Aright, I'll be waiting for you."

She knocked on his door, cracking the entrance to poke her head inside. "Grandfather?"

She could smell a soup bubbling on the stove in the kitchen, so she made her way through the cabin and out the back door. Grandfather sat in his garden, cross-legged, eyes closed. She stopped, waiting for him to acknowledge her.

"Granddaughter," he said after several minutes. "They tell me business in the office has been grim these past few days."

The bottom of her stomach felt sour, as if she'd eaten spoiled food- some of it still stuck on the way down.

"Why, Grandfather? Why steal from the family? From all the families in the Territory?"

He rose, and she was reminded of how tall he was, despite the leanness of his frame. When he looked at her, his bear peeked out of his eyes, the skin of his face tight.

"Steal? I do not steal what belongs to me. My fathers made this Territory a prosperous one."

Bewildered, she said, "But what do you need the money for, Grandfather? We have everything we need."

"We do not have power, the power we need to keep our land untainted by the pale faces who come up from the city, analyzing our land for the riches it might bring them." His shoulders swelled, hands thickening, voice deepening. "One day they will ask the Elders to open our land to their development, and Fire Eagle will have the power to stop it."

"And you think the way to get that power is through treachery?" The bruise on her heart hardened, along with her voice and expression.

"Grandfather, I'm taking over leadership of the Clan. I, as The Bear's Mate, will be the Fire Eagle Elder. That is the consequence for dishonoring our name, and our family."

He roared. Annina had not gotten her ability to shift in seconds from her father's family- but from her mother's father. Which was why she was his true Heir, his second.

Massive claws swiped at her head. Annina, in a certain amount of disbelief- even when he shifted to Bear, she hadn't really expected him to attack her- began her own shift. She flung herself to the side, tearing through the change to defend herself. But he shoved past her and was gone, the swift, heavy footsteps of a bear rocking the very foundation of the small house. She heard dual roars outside- Kavanaugh's human voice in response to Grandfather's, warning not to pursue. But Kavanaugh didn't pursue- he came running through the house shouting her name. Annina was already shifting back to human, dazed a bit from the knock to her head when she'd inadvertently flung herself onto a stone garden wall.

"Annina! Are you alright?"

He knelt next to her, patting her body with anxious hands, calm face struggling to hold sway over his angry face.

"I'm fine. Grandfather-" she swallowed. "I told him I'm taking over the Clan. What are you doing here?"

"Zeke told me where you were going- I didn't like it."

Because he had known, or at least suspected. Annina closed her eyes. "I've been so blind."

He brushed her head with his lips. "No, you love him. And sometimes we are willing to forgive the people we love even when we know they are wrong."

She opened her eyes then, regarding him steadily. "You're not mad at me?"

"No." And then he pulled away, drawing his habitual stillness around him like a shrug. "But I'm afraid you are going to be mad at me."

Annina rose to shaky feet. "Why Kavanaugh? What did you do?"

"I ceded the charters to Blade."

CHAPTER EIGHT

Kavanaugh's betrayal crushed her, stealing breath and leeching energy. Sleep eluded her, failure taunting her even in her dreams, Grandfather asking why he'd been betrayed for nothing. Annina might now lead the Clan, but the territory was no longer the Clan's to guide.

"Nina, you have to get out of bed," her cousin Halcione prodded her. "This isn't healthy. And you can't keep ignoring Clan business. I've kept everyone away for days now- I can't hold them off any longer."

"I'm tired," Annina said, voice dragging. Halcione pulled the comforter away from her limp hands.

"Get up now!" Halcione roared.

Annina started. Halcione never shouted. She pushed herself up on shaky arms, swinging legs over the side of the bed only to sink back down, dizzy.

"I told you I'm tired," Annina said, weakly. "I just can't seem to sleep these days. I think I may have the flu, too."

The younger female moved around the bed, placing a hand on Annina's forehead.

"This isn't simple tiredness. Do you think you're pregnant? You're scent is all wacky these days- I can't really tell."

She couldn't believe it hadn't occurred to her. Annina's heart stopped, started again, racing so fast she had to catch her breath- while sitting.

"Nina, calm down. Come on, girl, don't hyperventilate. Take deep breaths."

She heard Hal swear, also a rare occurrence, a moment later a glass of water appearing underneath her nose.

"Drink this."

Ann obeyed, the act of drinking the water clearing some space in her mind to think. She finished the glass, calming.

"I should get a test."

Halcione nodded. "We'll go together." She hesitated. "Um… Zeke brought me over here. He's waiting outside."

Annina stared at her cousin, horrified. "What? You traitor!"

Her cousin's slender shoulders hunched. "Listen, I can't help if you and Kavanaugh are having problems. That really doesn't have anything to do with me and-"

"There shouldn't *be* a you and Zeke."

She sighed. "I'm not arguing with a pregnant fear. Hey, hey. Are you crying?"

Annina sniffled. "No."

"My God. Come on, let's get you dressed. Some sunshine will do you good."

Hal was right as usual. The sun did make her feel better- cleared her mind and started her blood flowing again. They discussed the Clan business Halcione had been handling for the last several days on Annina's behalf- telling everyone that she was focused on finding Grandfather, leaving daily affairs to Hal. Annina realized her cousin had saved her a great deal of face- she couldn't afford to look weak. Especially when weak was exactly how she had behaved. Mate troubles or no, as Clan Elder she couldn't allow her personal life to affect business any longer.

She made several calls to family members and the offices- now somewhat in limbo since they were no longer handling the fishing contracts. Annina let them know to continue maintaining the family's various investments and rental properties and that a meeting would be called very soon to discuss the future.

They pulled up to the pharmacy, the sound of a familiar roar trailing them. Halcione took Annina's arm as the curvy woman began to turn, eyes narrowed.

"That sounds like Zeke," Annina said. "Hal, why is Zeke following us?"

"Just come on, Ann. We can fuss at him some other time."

"How is she?" Kavanaugh asked his second.

He stood next to Zeke's bike, sipping a triple shot of espresso because even if he was The Bear, Overlord of this mountainous, forest territory by Council decree- he still had to fight weariness, too. Sometimes. His normal unflagging energy began to fail him this week, and he could only attribute it to advancing age. He wasn't young, even in shifter terms. Annina might be shocked to learn just how much older than her he really was.

Kav glanced at Zeke then paused, staring him down. Lowering the coffee cup, "Zeke?"

Pale eyes slanted his way and his cousin shifted- a tell that immediately put Kavanaugh on the alert.

"Zeke," he growled. He knew the male better than he knew himself. "How is she?"

"She isn't sleeping well," the blond enforcer replied, evasively. "I can tell she's unhappy. Hal says-"

"Hal?"

Zeke's discomfort vanished. He straightened on the bike, turning his shoulders to face Kav.

"None of your business."

They locked glares. "That 'none of your business' is my mate's favorite cousin," The Bear warned quietly. "And a sweet girl from what I can tell."

"You don't have to warn me off," Zeke snapped. "I'm not going to dishonor her."

"Then what are your intentions?"

Zeke looked away. "She... is soothing."

Kavanaugh considered that. Also considered what Zeke didn't say. "But she isn't your mate."

"Does it matter? I'm not a slave to my biology- not everyone meets their mate. My 'mate' could live in Taiwan."

"That would be unfortunate. It's a hostile Territory to your kind."

"The point," Zeke said through gritted teeth, "is that she doesn't have to be my mate for me to claim her."

Kav turned back to watch the entrance of the pharmacy. "No. And maybe it's better that way," he said, almost to himself. "It gives you... space."

"What's it like? The mating bond?"

Kav couldn't answer right away. Wasn't sure there really were words to describe it.

"If I were a weaker man, the force of her personality would consume me." He smiled, wry and grim. "I... find myself working to separate her impressions from mine."

Zeke blew out a breath. "Yeah. Ain't feelin' that, man."

Kav didn't have much choice but to 'feel' it. "You haven't answered my question about Halcione."

"We're getting to know each other, alright? Damn. Shouldn't her father be grilling me?"

"Who better than her cousin's mate?"

Zeke stared up into the sky, face set. "I think... if she'll have me, I'll keep her."

Kav said nothing, hand tightening around his coffee. "Then we're both now invested in making this territory work."

"Yeah."

"And Annina?"

Zeke sighed. "I think she's pregnant."

Hot coffee exploded as The Bear crushed the cup in his hand.

Annina stumbled, holding her suddenly pounding temple.

"What's wrong?" Hal asked, alarmed.

"It's - I think it's Kavanaugh. He's..." she didn't want to say angry because that was not, precisely, what she felt from him. Anger, worry, shock, a surge of possessiveness and utter confusion before the sensations cut off.

"He's what?"

She shook her head. "Never mind. Let's just get this kit and go, I need to lie down."

It wasn't that simple- who knew there were so many different kinds of pregnancy tests? A clerk took pity on the females and helped them select the right kind. Annina grabbed the test and a pack of the driest looking shortbread cookies from the cracker aisle and paid. They hurried out of the store, stopping short when Hal caught sight of the two males.

"Nina."

Annina's head swung around- she'd felt his presence like a wall of Kavanaugh shaped energy by her side. Her insides clicked, the spark preceding blue flame before the punch of his presence activated the simmering desire she'd held at bay- mostly through sleep. But even in her dreams, she felt his arms around her, his steel inside her sheath. They stared at each other one long moment, the expression on his face queer, eyes steely.

As if her anger and resentment were buried behind a brick wall that suddenly caved, aggression surged to the surface. Her rational mind batted away in a tide of fury. Annina set her legs, drawing herself up to a height aided by shifter genetics, and roared.

The sound rippled through the lot, setting off alarms and startling birds from nearby trees. The roar shattered the last of her self-control, and she charged, the instincts of a threatened bear in the forefront. Dimly, she recognized the set of Kavanaugh's shoulders as he planted his feet hard enough in the cement that tiny cracks spread from his soles.

She rammed into him and he caught her around the shoulders, spinning them so the momentum of her tackle didn't send them crashing to the ground. His arms around her were strong but only human whereas she'd called on her Bear to augment her strength. Her paw swiped at his face, missing only because he grasped her wrist and slung her away from him. He roared finally, and when she regained her footing Annina began to shift, calling her full form in seconds, her ability to change rapidly a gift of her line. Bending over, fur began to spread across her arms, fangs- elongating where human blunt teeth had rested.

Annina! You'll kill the cub!

It was the only thing he could have said to stop her. The only emotion stronger than her desire to smash him for his betrayal was her instinct to protect her unborn baby. Her mind cleared a bit, enough for her human personality to broach the fury, and she clawed her way back to her fully human form, feeling as if she'd just run a marathon.

She heard the murmur of human voices and looked up. A few faces, wary, watched her. Keys dangling in hands as the last car alarm shut off, leaving only the sounds of the morning. Kavanaugh stood several feet away, arms outstretched as if to intercept her if she charged the humans. Why would she? They hadn't betrayed her. He had.

"Are you yourself?" he asked.

She licked her lips, knees shaking, and nodded.

"We need to talk, little bear."

It took her two tries to speak. "I don't want to talk to you."

Then she walked wide around him, avoiding his gaze and slamming shut her mental barriers, leading a silent Hal to the car.

"You didn't say anything to Zeke, did you? How did Kavanaugh know?" Annina asked once they were seat belted in. Her fingers trembled on the steering wheel, her own nature having shocked her. Annina couldn't remember a time she'd ever felt so… dangerous.

"No," Hal replied. "But did you really think you could keep something like this from your mate?"

"Yes."

She could, and she would. She'd gone into the contract knowing that there was a chance she would have a fatherless cub by the end of the year and day term- it had happened before to the poor concuines offered to an overlord when he came to a Territory. It would happen again.

After returning home, Annina shut herself in the bathroom with the kit, reading and rereading the instructions. Glad she hadn't already peed this morning because it said not to. Taking a deep breath, she waited the longest two minutes of her life, taking her time to wash her hands and straighten her hair. When it was time, she glanced down at the test sitting on the counter. Compared the indicator to the picture on the box.

Her heart stumbled, her knees collapsed and she sat down, hard, on the edge of the tub.

"Hal?" she called weakly. Forcing the words through her throat reminded her of a dream where no matter how hard she'd tried, she wasn't able to talk above a whisper. "Hal?"

"I'm here," her cousin said, entering the bathroom. Halcione took one look at Annina's face and sighed.

"You're pregnant."

"Yes."

She stood there, a gentle smile blooming on her lovely face. "Oh, Nina. A baby. The first baby of all the cousins our age."

Halcione bent at the waist and enveloped Annina in an awkward hug. "Come on, let's fix a light lunch, and just... relax. We have thirty-two weeks to figure out the details."

In the end, Annina found she didn't want to stay in the apartment. She felt claustrophobic, odd for a Bear, and wanted sunshine. Fresh air and birdsong to cheer her up. Worry gnawed at her, and protectiveness even as she dealt with the pain of her breakup.

"When are you going to tell him?"

"I'm not. Besides, he already thinks he knows."

Halcione sighed. They sat on crates in the greenhouse- the door wide open to allow in plenty of air circulation since neither of them knew if breathing in so much of the herb Hal was cultivating for the pharmaceutical manufacturer was harmful. It was certainly... fragrant.

"You know you-"

"I don't want to talk about it anymore."

They sat in silence for several minutes before Hal rose. "Well, since we're here we might as well go over the paperwork I received the other day contracting the family land for cultivation of the herb."

"Does it have a name?"

Halcione waved a hand. "Yes, but why bother trying to pronounce it? I just call it 'the herb."

"Aren't you a botanist? Shouldn't you be able to pronounce its name?"

"Botanist is not linguist. Let me go to the shed, I'll be right back."

They spent a good hour arguing over the terms, brainstorming who they could involve in cultivation and harvesting. Halcione admitted that the output the corporation wanted far exceeded the samples currently growing in her greenhouse.

"We'll have to clear a few acres," Annina mused. "Far enough away from the main roads that casual passerby's can't see, but not so far it's a pain in the ass to get to." She sighed, rubbing her head. "This is going to be a headache, but I have to admit- it's an income that we won't have to fight over every five years. On our land."

Halcione beamed. "See? Didn't I tell you- what's that smell?"

They rose, senses on the alert as a sudden waft of burnt fertilizer odor came into the greenhouse. Annina turned towards the direction of the wind, frowning.

"Hal-"

The explosion ripped through the heavy plastic and thin wood frame of the greenhouse, a fiery chemical smoke that flung them backwards and stung Annina's eyes. Bears were hardy even in human form, but when she fell back, head cracking against one of the cinder block planters holding down plastic at the end of the house, she lost consciousness.

And woke, the smell of smoke in her nostrils, a sticky wetness at her head. Plants consumed by flame in seconds, the wooden plant boxes burning with a thick, heavy smoke. Melting plastic.

Annina.

Hearing a low moan, Annina forced her eyes to open, wincing from the chemical burn, rolling onto her stomach to push up on her elbows.

"Kavanaugh?" Were her ears playing tricks on her?

Annina, where are you?

And then she realized the sick feeling in her stomach, the turmoil of anger and fear wasn't just hers. Feeling her mate claw his way past her natural mental barriers, she relaxed some of her resistance, allowing him in. The force of his mind flooding hers was like hitting her head on a log in a raging river. Blackness enveloped her again.

Annina, Annina. Wake up.

The insistent chanting in her head brought her back to consciousness. Somehow, she didn't think more than a few minutes had passed.

"You're giving me a headache," she muttered.

His presence receded, then approached her with more care.

Where are you?

Hal's greenhouse. Bomb- I think.

Annina, I need you to get out of the greenhouse. The smoke could make the cub sick. I smell it.

She pushed up onto her knees, gasping because even that movement spun the insides of her head.

"Hal?"

"Here," a faint reply came. "Gotta get out of here."

Annina coughed, struggling to inhale clean air.

"Don't get up, crawl," Hal said, voice scratchy. "Hurry."

"You okay?"

"Just go."

Annina crawled as it occurred to her that they could be crawling right into the arms of whatever enemy flung the bomb.

"Hal, whoever-"

"I know."

But they couldn't stay in the burning greenhouse. It been only a matter of minutes, but any longer could kill them. Humans would have been dead from smoke inhalation.

Hal made it to a panel of plastic yet untouched by flame. Her hand shaped into a paw with sharp claws, tearing rivulets through the plastic to allow them to crawl out. Tears streamed from Annina's eyes as she gulped the fresh- fresher- air. Halcione wrapped an arm around Annina's waist, tugging her to her feet. She knew she was wounded, just didn't know how, and scented the tang of blood and crisped flesh that wasn't hers, so she knew Hal was hurt as well. They ran, crouched at the waist, to the tree line, hoping they weren't running into danger.

Once clear of the greenhouse by several yards, they found a copse of thick bushes to rest beneath.

"Wait for Kav," Hal whispered.

"Ahead of you," Annina said, forgetting to wonder how Hal knew Kavanaugh was coming.

CHAPTER NINE

She must have lost consciousness again. She woke to a gentle tapping on her cheek and an insistent voice calling her name.

"Annina, I need you to wake up."

Her eyes pried themselves open. Though sluggish, she knew she shouldn't have let herself sleep. Something about head injuries and sleeping.

"Kavanaugh."

Strong arms lifted her, cradling her against a rock hard chest. His voice rumbled against her ear, lips brushing against her uninjured forehead.

"I've got you, sweeting. Zeke has Halcione. You'll both be fine."

Annina struggled to think. "She's hurt."

She turned her head toward the sound of near silent feet, saw Zeke glance at her. Annina didn't know if it was the combination of tears and debris in her eyes, but his face looked...strange. Nearly reptilian, pale eyes long and flat. Annina blinked, and he turned away.

"We'll take care of it," Kavanaugh said. "Stay awake, Ann."

"Okay."

She did, mostly, drifting in and out of full awareness, so tired, her nose, throat and eyes sore and stinging. A sharp throbbing in the back of her head causing her teeth to clench. It should have healed by now- oh, wait. She was pregnant. That meant she healed slower, her body's resources diverted to the baby. The baby.

"Kavanaugh!" She began to struggle, instinctively.

He cursed. "Ann, calm down, you have a concussion, and you inhaled a good amount of toxic chemical along with that plant of Hal's- which may or may not be hallucinogenic."

"Baby!"

"We're taking you to a doctor. Just calm down."

And he sent a wash of soothing calm trough their bond, helping her settle and dampened her worry. And sleep. Distantly, she heard him curse, and smiled. Guess he'd done a whoopsie.

Annina remembered the doctor's office vaguely, talks of increased healing times and the mysterious properties of the herb she and Hal inhaled. Hal down the hall, alert and angry, voice animated. Cool gel on her belly and the press of smooth plastic.

"Baby is fine," Kav said, smoothing her hair back from her head during one of her more lucid moments. "And you just have to sleep off the effects of that smoke. Doc said your head is healing clean, just slow. Go to sleep now."

She woke the next morning, the familiar scent of her mate surrounding her, though she knew he wasn't beside her in the bed.

Sitting up, Annina touched the back of her head gingerly, feeling freshly healed, slightly puckered skin. In another day, it should be perfectly smooth. She'd have to have a talk with her mother about pregnancy- something they'd never really discussed in depth before, since there had always seemed to be time.

Swinging her legs out of the bed, as soon as her feet touched the floor Annina knew she'd slept off the remains of the smoke. She felt rested even, and for a week now her energy had lagged.

A shower was the next order of business, then clean clothing. She emerged from the bedroom, intent on getting into town and seeing Halcione. Whoever had made it their business to attack the Fire Eagle Clan head- though, to be fair, it wasn't common knowledge yet that Annina had taken over the Clan- was about to get the full brunt of the family brought down on their head.

Kavanaugh stepped into the hall as Annina came down the stairs. She started, having not felt or heard him. Proof of her own focus on the hunt. Annina stopped short, staring at him.

"We need to talk," he said.

"I'm aware you're scheduling meetings with all the Clan heads," she replied, stiffly. "I'd appreciate if you would detain mine, for a week or two. As you saw- we have some pressing business to take care of."

He slammed his fist through the plaster. Annina jumped back, almost stumbling on the stairs before she caught herself, furious at her reaction. She wasn't a frightened child, but a Clan leader.

"What the fuck?"

He withdrew his hand from the wall, slowly, hard eyes holding hers. His knuckles bled, bits of paint and plaster falling to the floor.

"Don't," he said, "dismiss me. Ever again."

"I wasn't dismissing you." Ice would have melted on her tongue. "And if you put your fist in a wall near me again- my Clan will consider it a declaration of threat, and respond accordingly."

"What is wrong with you? I thought my mate was mature, strong spirited. I see a bitter child in front of me."

Taken aback, her anger spurred her down the remaining steps. He had temper- she had temper.

"Bitter, or spurned?" She pushed past him, deliberately bumping his shoulder with her own. "Don't worry, Eldest. You won't have to deal with this bitter child except on official business. Which I'll try to make as little as possible."

He grabbed her wrist as she passed, yanking her to a stop. As she exclaimed in fury he swept her up into his arms- and this time a fully aware Annina struggled.

"Put. Me. Down."

"Gladly."

But he just dropped her on the overstuffed leather couch, pinning her with the full length of his body, hands on either side of her head, dark eyes glassy chips of obsidian, hard and jagged.

"I know you're upset about the charters- I've given you enough time to cool off. But this pettiness of yours is going to come to an end. Now. You have an obligation to fulfill."

Was he insane? "*Obligation?* You're the one who-"

He kissed her. The texture of his lips felt like frustration and restless desire, one provocation away from being slated in her body whether she willed it or no. Her back arched involuntarily, pelvis grinding into him as she felt the rapid hardening of his cock pressing against her.

"This is the only thing that shuts you up," he said. "That soothes your infernal pigheadedness. But I can't keep my cock in your pussy all day. I need you to grow up a little. I gave Blade the charters. I didn't shun you. Separate yourself- us- from territory business for just one damn second in your stubborn head."

Annina shut her open mouth, listening to his words. It was the rawest, the most open, she'd ever heard him. And, if she were honest with herself, the best way to handle her. A kiss and plain speaking. Desire burned through her haze of resentment, softening her heart and allowing her mind to think with more neutrality as she considered the reasons for her anger at him.

When it had come time for ratification of lucrative fishing contracts her family had overseen for generations, Kavanaugh had yanked them from Fire Eagle control and given them to Annina's worst enemy, Terrence Blade. A Clan bent on Fire Eagle demise. She'd considered it Kavanaugh's way of telling her that he no longer wanted her for consort. By siding against her family, he'd chosen not to fulfill her Boon.

"What do you want?" Annina asked.

"I want what I've always wanted. My mate." His expression softened, just a little. "My cub."

"You gave the charters to Blade."

"I freed you from an unhealthy obsession. Freed your grandfather from facing charges by the Council."

The words chilled her. It was something she had never considered- and immediately understood would lead to her grandfather's execution. The Council could not abide thieves, many of them hailing from countries and centuries where the punishment for stealing was something permanent, and maiming.

"Fine."

He stared at her, frustration forming a small line between his brows.

"What do you mean, 'fine?'"

She bucked her hips, impatient. "I mean, fine. I accept your apology."

"I didn't-" he stopped. "Thank you, sweeting. For accepting my... apology."

She nodded grudgingly. "Just don't do it again. I might not be so forgiving next time you betray me so heinously."

Kavanaugh said nothing.

After several moments underneath his cool, calculating gaze, Annina began to squirm.

"Why are you staring at me?" she demanded, voice hot. "Stop it."

He smiled slowly, knowingly. His head dipped, eyes trained on hers even as his lips brushed hers once, twice. His teeth nipping at her lips with increasing pressure.

"Ow," she gasped when he drew a bead of blood.

"My bad."

Kavanaugh straightened, hauling her up with him by her wrists. She tumbled against his chest, stomach pressed into his hard cock. She almost couldn't breathe he held her so tight, one hand caressing down her back to cup and pinch her plump buttocks, massaging the flesh until her head tilted back and she moaned. It was one of her favorite touches besides his mouth on her neck, made her body warm, vibrating with need.

"Turn around, Annina," he said, releasing her.

"What?"

He didn't repeat himself, just looked at her. She licked her lips, turning slowly, felt him back up several steps.

"Now take off the pants. Slowly."

"Kav-"

"Do it!" His voice whipped her, brooking no defiance.

Unsnapping the button of her jeans, she hooked her thumbs in the waistband and pushed them down over her hips, twisting so she could look over her shoulder at the same time. He watched her, hunger bright in his gaze. Though she couldn't tell if he wanted to fuck- or feed.

Her breath came faster. She began to lift a leg to completely remove the jeans.

"No," he said. "Bend over and do it."

"Kav-"

"If you argue one more time," he replied in a silky croon, "I will punish you, Annina. You certainly deserve it for attacking me. You don't want me to punish you. "

Maybe she did, if it would feel anything like his voice did, rough and sexual, sending a shiver of sparks dancing over her spine. She felt her panties dampen as she obeyed him, bending over slowly, widening her legs just a little, pushing the jeans off her feet and tossing them to the side. She arched the small of her back so her rounded bottom stuck in the air.

Kavanaugh approached, his fingers trailing over the cheeks of her ass, underneath her panties- and delving into her folds without warning, fingers pushing inside her pussy with a near punishing force, bringing a gasp to her throat.

Hands flat on the floor for balance, Annina mewled as he finger fucked her, three of his large, strong digits opening her canal and preparing her for an even larger entry. Then she watched as he dropped to his knees, prying her thighs apart even further. He pushed the panties down her legs, then ripped them off, impatiently- she'd learned weeks ago to wear flimsy fabric because he seemed to enjoy tearing off her underwear. She'd replaced all her briefs and boy shorts and hadn't gone back to wearing them during the break up.

"Shhh," he said. "I'm not really fucking you yet. This is just a tease."

"More."

"Did you miss this, Annina?" He pinched her ass, punishment for her silence.

"Yes," she cried out. "Yes, I missed you."

He laughed, dark and humorless. "Not enough, though. I think I'm going to remind you of the benefits of being mine- and the punishment for leaving me."

When his tongue reached between her folds and found her clit, she moaned, nails digging into the wood floor in her pleasure. He spread her lips with his fingers, fully exposing her clit to him as he lapped up and down her slit, suckling on her nub until her knees quivered. When his tongue delved into her pussy, Annina thought her knees would collapse.

"Kavanaugh, please, I need you," she said, near pleading.

He rose, pushing her forward onto the couch, positioning her so she draped over the back, the plush cushions soft on her middle. The metal click of the zipper preceded his thick cock rubbing across her ass before the soft head nudged her entrance. She arched her ass up as much as possible, angling so the when he slid into her, one inexorable inch at a time, the angle of his cock in her pussy pressed hard against her pelvis bone.

The Bear rumbled as he slid all the way in, sheathing himself until his balls were snug against her ass. Instead of pulling out, he began to rock his hips, grinding so deep inside her she screamed from the pressure, rearing back into him. He wrapped an arm around her middle, his free hand gripping the couch for leverage as he fucked him. She clawed at his arms, the pleasure pain driving her mad. Kavanaugh changed his rhythm, sliding out, drenched in her juices, then slamming back in. A harsh, nearly punishing move of his hips.

"Kav!"

"Pleasure and pain, Annina. Reward and punishment."

His fucked her fast and raw, showing no mercy as he slid in and out with the strength of Bear, finding her spot and using her own body against her. She cried and begged for him to stop, for him to give her more. When her orgasm crested and spilled from her she felt drained, limp, even as he continued to fuck her, wringing his own pleasure from her well-used pussy.

Kavanaugh's hand wrapped around her neck, turning her head so he could kiss her, deep and drugging.

"Remember," he said hoarsely. "The next time you want to leave me."

CHAPTER TEN

"I know you think I know, like, everything," Zeke said in his most sarcastic valley girl voice, "but I'm not a bomb expert."

Hal knelt in the wreckage of the smoldering greenhouse, sniffing. "I can identify most of the chemicals used," she said. "A standard garden bomb... ammonium nitrates, fuel, and a few other things to make it interesting. The detonator would have to have been a good ways from the greenhouse. They must have taken it with them."

Zeke snarled, a sound between a hiss and a yowl. Annina stared at him, the hairs on the back of her neck rising to attention. Her fingers spasmed, claws pricking in her nail beds before she grabbed hold of her bear. It was the... eeriest thing she'd ever heard.

"What are you?" she wondered aloud.

Zeke smiled, though it wasn't necessarily friendly. Her hackles rose.

"Stop it," Kav said. "She bites."

Rising to her feet, Hal brushed off her palms, staring at the ashed plants, expression set.

"When I find out who did this," she said, "I'm going to kill them."

Her tone arrested Annina's smart reply to the males. The anger simmering under Hal's voice... she'd never heard it before. Had always understood there was more to her cousin's seemingly soft personality than at the surface. She felt as if she'd just caught a glimpse of something... bigger. Annina watched her carefully, considering the future. Having shoved the problem of who to appoint as her second to the back of her mind days ago, Annina now filed away the new information to analyze at a later date.

Zeke assessed Hal as well, a cool expression in his eyes that chilled Annina. The cool expression of a professional killer, determining the worth of a new recruit.

"I can help you with that," he said. "But we have to find him first."

"Wait a minute," Annina objected. "I don't want Hal involved in this."

The three looked at Annina. She stared back at them, baffled by the gravity in their expressions.

"Is that a command, Elder?" Halcione asked.

Annina blinked, thrown. "Uh..."

"Don't give orders unless you mean them," The Bear advised. "It will only confuse your people."

"Oh." This time when Annina studied her cousin, it was with the eyes of Clan Elder, and not cousin.

"You'll be with her?" Fire Eagle's Elder asked The Bear's Enforcer.

"Yes," the Enforcer replied.

"Alright," Annina said, sighing. "Just be careful."

"Hard, isn't it?" Kav said. "Sending a liege into danger."

Her lips tightened. He didn't have to rub it in, though when she glanced at him again, the empathy and perception in his clear eyes let her know he wasn't rubbing it in- but commiserating as an experienced leader to a newbie.

Whatever drama was going on around them, the territory still required a certain amount- well, most- of Kavanaugh's attention. He had to leave his mate and her cousin in the hands of Zeke. He knew the man would guard them both with his life, while allowing the women to feel their way as the leaders of their Clan. Annina might just be realizing what Kavanaugh already knew- she had a second in Halcione whose loyalty and spine would be an asset in decades to come. Not all strength required wielding in the form of a big stick. Sometimes a light touch engendered similar results, without all the bruises.

Terrence Blade waited for him at the office, sprawled in a lobby chair with the air of someone who'd been waiting, quite comfortably, for a time. Kavanaugh refrained from waving a hand in front of his face, merely propped open the door to allow some of the smoke to flee. Terrence grinned around his pipe.

"Thought this place could use some character," the Blade Clan Elder said. "How's the Fire wench?"

Kavanaugh supposed he needed some kind of receptionist to man the office while he was gone. Ignoring the male's casual insult of Kavanaugh's mate, he strode down the hall, leaving it up to Blade to follow or not. Terrence was the type who enjoyed needling people just to see them snap and snarl.

Though, in this case, Kavanaugh couldn't really blame the man. Annina was ferocious in her... single-minded insistence that Terrence Blade was responsible for everything wrong with her Clan, the territory and the known universe. Exhausting, trying to get her to see reason while not looking as if he were trying to get her to see reason. Fortunately, she seemed to be developing a wider worldview. Which lightened his burden considerably. He hadn't wanted to take the Clan Leadership away from her, but if her stubbornness led the territory into war... now Kavanaugh was fairly confident he could leave her alone to grow into the power she'd seized. Mistakes would always be made, that was the nature of ruling any group of people, but those kinds of mistakes would teach the kind of valuable lessons which only served to make one stronger.

"My mate is well," Kavanaugh replied when Blade meandered in the office after him. The Bear sat behind his desk, watching as Blade pulled up a seat, crossing his ankle at the knee, pipe dangling from the side of his mouth.

"Got her pregnant yet?"

Kavanaugh blinked. He wasn't entirely... certain... how to respond. Blade watched him shrewdly.

"You got the look of a male bent on settling down," Terrence said. "I've seen it before- of course, it usually doesn't take a Bear several decades past his first century, though."

He wasn't surprised the Blade Elder knew- or had some idea of- his true age. Terrence had been around quite a bit longer, after all.

"Hmm. Anyhow, what I came by for was to show you this."

Terrence brushed aside one of his long, beaded braids, reaching inside the pocket of his quilted jacket to pull out a folded manila envelop. He tossed it on the desk.

Kavanaugh opened it, pulling out a sheaf of photocopied papers, eyes skimming over the contents rapidly.

"Where did you get this?" The Bear asked, eyes brightening to an amber glow.

Terrence sat, unperturbed. "Front porch yesterday morning. Didn't know what to make of it." A few puffs of the pipe. "You didn't know."

He'd wondered what all the little plants- well, ashes of plants- in Halcione's greenhouse were for when the female had described its properties to the doctor. He wasn't a botanist- but he'd understood she was growing something a bit more exotic than cooking herbs and vegetables, though from the conversation the plant was indigenous to the region. Halcione just hadn't mentioned why she'd been growing it, and he had pushed the matter aside as unimportant. A careless mistake- he'd assumed the bomb was because of Annina. Now he wasn't certain.

"We've been... distracted."

"Heard an explosion in the mountains, up around Fire Eagle land."

Kavanaugh made a decision. "A bomb was set off in a greenhouse containing these plants. Halcione has been growing them."

"Makes sense." The Elder nodded at the papers. "I don't like an outsider trying to play one Clan against another to get an economic advantage."

"They don't want Fire Eagle to have the leverage of being their only supplier. You think they set the bomb to buy Blade time to create some competition."

"Don't want to jump to conclusions. What kind of bomb? I smelled the smoke."

"Halcione said it was made of things one could purchase from a garden store."

"Eh. Not too fancy then? Seems like a big drug company would be a bit more spiffy in their bullying tactics."

"Maybe not." Kavanaugh's fingers drummed on the desk. "You choose your tactics based on your enemy. Halcione doesn't require fancy bullying where simple will do."

Blade grunted. "Outsiders don't know them girls then. Mean tempered little grizzly bi-"

Kavanaugh growled. Terrence just laughed, standing up. "I'll nose around a bit, see who else in my family these outclan may have spoken to." Blade's eyes sparked. "And if I find any of mine were involved..."

The Bear figured Blade wouldn't call him to take care of that problem.

Annina parked the SUV at the lodge and made her way into the mountains. It was time to find Grandfather. She'd hoped he would return-anything could be forgiven. As the days passed, she feared he might have lost his humanity to the Bear. Succumbed, finally, to the neurological condition that sapped his rational thinking skills and memory with increasing frequency.

When she'd confronted him several days ago after finding out he'd deliberately embezzled profits from the fishing contracts, it hadn't been with the intent of punishment, but only to get him to see that Annina taking over the Clan was the best for everyone. So far,

Blade hadn't spearheaded a demand for restitution from Fire Eagle- though she had her accountants looking into that so whatever remained of the funds could be returned as soon as possible. The land purchased with the funds either sold or divided between the area families in various Clans in order to make sure the wealth was redistributed as it should have been.

They were meant to be caretakers of the Territory's resources, not owners.

She shouldered a pack. As a Bear, it was possible to hunt and find water but with the pregnancy in such early stages, she didn't want to tax her body unnecessarily with a shift. In fact, it was recommended shifter women not change for at least the first trimester. Fortunately, she wasn't a wolf, slave to the dictates of the full moon.

Making her way deeper into the forest, there came a point where rolling hills met an abrupt incline. Hiking, at that point, became a reality rather than a casual activity. Steep enough she had to be careful of her hand and footholds, she approached the series of caves the family made home away from home when on four claws. Near a large stream, the location was an ideal one. The stream was wide and

EMMA ALISYN

deep enough for fishing, both in human and
bear form. Years ago, they'd planted additional
berry shrubs and edible wild greens to
supplement what grew naturally. Food, shelter,
water... there was no better place for
Grandfather to be staying.

Approaching the entrance of one of the
caves, she called out his name, entering the
cave with eyes she shifted to bear to aid her
vision. After a thorough search of that cave and
its neighbors, she knew Grandfather hadn't
been there. The typical signs of disturbance
were missing, and she scented no recent
occupants. She sat down on a bolder by the
stream, energy flagging, wondering what to do
next. The sun was beginning to set, and she
was hungry. She didn't have much of a taste for
raw fish- or for camping. Besides, since they'd
more or less made up, Kavanaugh was
probably expecting her to come... home.

Annina sat a few more minutes, sipping on
water and chewing a granola bar and a few
pieces of chocolate. Standing, she made her
way back down the mountain. She'd have to try
a different direction tomorrow. Again and again,
until she found her grandfather. Before it was
too late.

Burns were trickier than any other injury. Halcione felt the tight itchiness of her healing skin, trying to keep herself from bothering the new, pink layer. She shuddered. It didn't actually hurt anymore, but she could still feel the phantom pain all up and down her arm.

"What do you need?" Zeke asked.

He hadn't been entirely pleased to find her at the greenhouse, going through the rubble. But where was she going to go, what else was she going to do? She had gardens to see to- some portion of them had also been affected by the blast.

"Electric fences," she replied, then paused when he cast a serious eye around the cleared perimeter of her land, as if he were weighing it in his mind.

"Zeke, that was a joke."

"Huh. I prefer you stick close to town until I figure out who set the bomb."

She hesitated. It made sense and was a reasonable request. But if she were going to be Ann's second, she couldn't stick to safety.

"I can't do that," she said finally. "The family needs this income. I have to get back to work."

He folded his arms. "Sure, try working dead."

She smiled at him, stretching onto her toes to place a soft kiss on his cheek. His temper was sweet- she knew he was worried about her.

"I don't think it will come to that."

He stared at her, summer sky eyes unblinking. "Blade found a copy of the contracts on his porch with an interesting little note about future economic opportunities and all that."

Halcione felt the slow burn of her usually cool temper bubble, and overflow. Her eyes hardened. "That is a choice the outsiders will regret. I don't care for dishonesty."

"And what do you plan on doing about it?"

"I'm going to make them an offer they can't refuse."

CHAPTER ELEVEN

Annina was almost home when her cell rang. She dug it out of her pocket, glancing at the falling sun and cursing. What was it now?

"Annina," Kavanaugh said, tone brisk.

She tensed. "Yes?"

"Come to the office. Quickly, please."

"I'm on my way."

She cut off the call, changing her direction to head into town. Pulling up outside the office, the first thing she saw was the beat up old red truck belonging to Terrence Blade. Her lip curled back, a growl rumbling her chest before she managed to control herself. Over the last hour she'd done some hard thinking- the man was as aggravating as a gnat, and she could tick off at least a half dozen petty attempts at sabotage in council- but he'd never actually lied when caught.

The office door was locked. She rapped on the glass, looking through the darkened lobby and halls. A thin gleam of life shone from the closed door of The Bear's office. It opened, Kavanaugh emerging. He strode down the hall, expression closed.

"Annina, I want you to be reasonable," he said, once he let her in.

It was probably the wrong thing to say. He must have realized it as she pushed past him because she saw the subtle tightening of his jaw. He caught her wrist, swinging her around into his arms and kissing her thoroughly. Just as her body began to heat from the feel of his sculpted frame against her curves, he let go.

"Annina, I mean it. Be reasonable."

She stared at him. Turned and matched his stride down the hall. It was just wide enough for him to follow right on her heels. If they were both a bit younger, they would have been jostling for position. As it was- they came close.

Kavanaugh reached for the knob just as she did. She glared at him until his had inched back, then flung open the door.

Terence stood inside. Annina knew whatever the trouble it was series. His normally sardonic expression was absent, along with his pipe. Anger lurked in his eyes when his head turned towards her. She'd never seen him looking so... ageless. He carried himself with the straightness of a young man, the lines of his face smoothed until nearly nonexistent.

Her glance took in the young man standing in a corner, a teenager she recognized from Blade's family, near adulthood but not yet at the point where a passage ceremony should be called. His shoulders slumped, face covered by a fall of unbraided hair. Not even one braid with beads to indicate his Clan Elder acknowledged him as a useful member of society.

"Blade," she said.

His eyes narrowed, then glanced at her mate. "You didn't tell her."

Kavanaugh said nothing.

Terrence snorted. "I'll remember this. Come here, boy."

The teenager slunk forward, glancing up at Annina with an edge of defiance in his expression.

"This one's actions bring shame to the family," Blade said, the chilly note of finality in his tone almost causing Annina to take a step back. "Do with him what you will, Elder."

He acknowledged her as leader of her Clan, an equal. She could not return he acknowledgement with insult, or petty anger. She was not her Grandfather.

"What is he guilty of?"

"This cretin is the one who set the bomb that may have killed you and sister Halcione."

Annina stilled. Refused to speak for several long moments. Blade watched, eagle-eyed and equally still.

"Why?" she asked the boy.

"To bring food to my family table," he replied, resentment in his tone. "The outlanders said if the plants were destroyed then there would be more income for Blade."

She studied him. "Did you know we were in the greenhouse?"

He said nothing, shrugged jerkily.

"Did you know?"

"Does it matter?" he asked flatly. "Whether I knew is no excuse."

"You're owed restitution," Kavanaugh said, inflectionless. "I'll forgo my right to vengeance for the near death of my mate and cub in favor of Fire Eagle's claim."

"Cub?" the boy said, face turning... green.

Annina rubbed a hand over her face, suddenly weary. She had no desire to exact vengeance on a child- but it was not their way to allow youth to avoid the consequences of their actions- that wasn't how you produced a responsible adult.

"I'll have to think of what to do with you," she said. "What you did was more serious than destruction of property. You could have killed us."

"I didn't mean to."

"Your full intent will be taken into consideration. But-"

"I think I have a solution," Halcione said from the doorway.

Annina turned her head, a little surprised she hadn't heard her cousin and Zeke approach.

"Hal?"

Her cousin was staring at the teenager, eyes harder than Ann could recall seeing. She stepped into the room.

"A solution that will take care of his punishment- and the outsiders' for inciting a child to commit a crime."

They would have many more meetings before the details were ironed out- but the Clan leaders present left the office with a sense of satisfaction. Annina glimpsed a grudging respect in Blade's eyes before he shoved his pipe back in his mouth and ambled out of the office, cub dragged along by his scruff.

"This will only work if we remain united," Annina said.

Halcione sighed. "I suppose it was wrong to try and hoard what is a natural resource to our family alone. Our greed opened the door- but now that we've agreed to share in the labor and the profits, the corporation will have to deal with us as a whole."

Zeke grinned. "So you can price fix all you want."

Halcione's glance was reproving. "Our terms will be fair."

"What for?"

It was late by the time Annina and Kav walked through the door of the cabin. She went straight to the kitchen, opening the fridge and cabinets.

"I knew it," she said, sighing.

Kavanaugh leaned against the doorway, arms folded. She supposed that was his way of showing guilt.

"We didn't really have time to grocery shop. I'm sorry- I should have thought. I can run back into town and get a pizza or something."

She sat the kitchen table. "Yeah, that would be best. I spent all day hiking- I'm tired."

He frowned. "You're pregnant. Why are you hiking?"

Annina stared. "Pregnant doesn't mean sick. I was looking for my grandfather."

His eyes widened, arms dropping to his sides as he straightened to his full height. "What?"

Brown cheeks flushed in anger. "Don't you yell at me. He's sick. He needs-"

"To be left alone! He's gone were by now, Annina. I can't believe you were that stupid!"

She surged to her feet, hands slapping on the table as she leaned towards him. "You're damn right he's probably gone were- and it's my fault. If there's any chance for him to get better-"

"He is never going to get better, Annina." He stalked towards her, rounding the table to seize her by the arms, sticking his face in hers. "Do you understand? He was mentally ill even in human form- he chose to run off into the woods with what little sanity he had left. I forbid you to go after him."

She yanked herself out of his grip, even angrier because she knew if he'd wanted, he could have held her captive. At least in human form.

"You can't forbid me to do anything," she replied, voice cold. "I am the Fire Eagle Clan Elder. This is my land and here I am the one who does the forbidding, not you."

"You're an inexperienced girl carrying my cub," he growled. "And if you are one Elder among several- I am the overlord of you all. Don't forget to whom you speak."

Her look was withering. "I speak to a fool."

She brushed past him out of the kitchen, anger spurring her steps.

"Where are you going?" he asked.

"For a walk. If you're smart, you'll stay here." She heard his footsteps hard on her heels and whirled when she reached the front door. "I mean it, Kavanaugh- leave me alone. I am so angry I want to leave and never come back."

He took one long step away from her, eyes chilly. "Then go. I won't come after you."

Annina slammed the door behind her and dove into the woods surrounding the cabin, wishing she could leave and never come back. Wishing she could make some wild, dramatic gesture that would make him sorry for his words- but wouldn't harm anyone.

She walked, pushing herself hard enough that she managed to get a full mile from the cabin in less than fifteen minutes. But as her anger flagged, so did her energy. Foolish. No food in her, little water. An already long day hiking and even more emotionally taxing evening and here she was- taking another hike. She sank to her haunches, leaning against a tree, closing her eyes. Talk about too stupid to live.

If she were the heroine of a romance story this would be the moment she was attacked by a mountain lion, or something.

Annina?

Don't Annina me, she thought with a mental growl.

Annina.

His mind brushed hers, opening the mating bond to allow his consciousness to flow through to hers. She felt him sigh.

I'm an old man, little bear. Are you going to make me come to you?

I doubt you could. I followed no path.

His amusement was clear. She was becoming too tired to care.

There is nowhere you could go I wouldn't find you. Pause. Stay put. I'm bringing pizza. And chocolate cake.

That endeared him to her just a little, but she wondered how he was going to keep the pizza hot. She supposed if she'd made a mile in under fifteen, he could make it in under ten if he really wanted to. Especially in Bear form. But then he couldn't carry the picnic in his teeth. Her tired mind began to idly brainstorm various harnesses one could put on a bear. Giant fanny packs and messenger bags. The images were enough that she began to giggle, and then laugh, in the deep quiet of night.

The rustle of brush alerted her to the approach of a shifter. She recognized the weight of footsteps and rose, brushing off the seat of her pants.

That was quick, she thought at her mate. *It didn't take you long to get here.*

The quick snap of his awareness caused her to wince.

I'm not there, Annina.

What?

Annina-

A bear broke through the brush, head swinging towards her as if it already knew she was present. Annina recognized the iron gray and black fur, the patches of white on its paws.

"Grandfather," she called, taking several steps forward.

Annina! Back up slowly.

She froze. *It's Grandfather.*

I know. The grim finality of his mental voice chilled her. She looked at her grandfather again, this time with the eyes of an Elder, and not a Granddaughter. The Bear rose up onto its hind legs and roared.

Can you shift before he attacks?

Attacks? She didn't want to believe it, but when she looked in the Bear's eyes, she saw nothing left of her grandfather. She began to back away slowly.

"I don't know," she said aloud, calmly. Hoping her human voice would soothe any instincts to attack. "I'm going to try and leave the area now. I'm no threat. There's no reason for him to attack me."

But she placed her arms behind her back. She couldn't fully shift, but a trickle of energy changed her human hands into paws with claws, thickened her legs and middle with extra dense padding, just enough to protect her soft insides with the extra flesh and muscle.

"Grandfather," she said softly. "Please hear me. It's Annina. You can come home."

She backed up another step, heel catching on an unseen branch and sending her sprawling. Her arms flailed in the air for balance. The Bear saw her waving claws and roared again, dropping with an earth-shaking thud to all fours and charging.

Annina swallowed a curse and rolled to her feet with the speed of desperation and her were genetics, flinging herself at the nearest tree and climbing with born dexterity. With his weight, he could follow her maybe thirty meters- if she were fast she might be able to wait him out.

But she wasn't fast enough. A claw dug into her ankle as the tree shook, grabbing her and flinging her to the ground.

Annina screamed, the impact jarring the breath from her lungs. The Bear whirled, graceful even with its weight and reared up, preparing to stomp. She rolled as it came down on the ground, sucking in air and dirt. It swiped at her as she rolled, catching her vulnerable back with its claws. Her blood filled the air and Annina knew the scent would drive him mad. Him, it. Bear, Grandfather.

But it whined, backing away from her. She staggered to her feet, feeling the stickiness of blood pouring down her back.

I'm almost there, Annina. Just survive.

The Bear lifted its head in the air, sniffing. Pawed at the ground, whining.

"Grandfather?" She held her claws ready. He stood completely still, head tilted as he studied her. The mad glow of his eyes receded and she took a step forward, relieved.

"Grandfather!"

He reared up onto hind legs, roared, and then charged her again- but this time, when it reached her, his movements were slow, just slow enough that when he opened his muzzle wide to attack, she had time. Time to defend herself.

She might have closed her eyes, those last few seconds before his teeth came close to her neck, snapping as if to tear out the tender flesh. But she wanted to witness his last moments when her shifted claw swung, connecting with the sinew underneath the Bear's chin, slicing through vein and flesh. He didn't move, didn't defend himself. He dropped to the ground, blood pouring.

And when Kavanaugh burst through the trees, Grandfather was almost human again, the last of the beast receding as he shifted, throat torn away. She dropped to her knees beside him, unable to speak. Unable to cry. The brown of Grandfather's eyes returned and he looked at her, then smiled.

A long time later Kavanaugh pulled her to her feet, whispering nonsense words that barely registered.

"It isn't your fault," she heard from a distance. Later she would talk about the night with her mate, later they would realize Grandfather had allowed her final strike- and he would only have done that if he were aware how dangerous he was. He never would have wanted to hurt her if he was sane.

Grandfather's funeral pyre was the next day- it wasn't their way to suffocate their dead, or leave them in cold boxes for a week. The Clans gathered, the last rites drummed,

Grandfather's ashes allowed to disperse in the wind. At the funeral, Blade and Fire Eagle declared truce publicly and Annina vowed the death of her Elder wouldn't be for nothing.

Kavanaugh held her in his arms as she watched the last of the embers wink out. He stood behind her, his hands covering her belly protectively.

"One generation returns, and another emerges," he said softly. "His ashes will feed the earth that feeds us, and the earth that feeds our cub. He isn't gone, little bear."

She pulled his arms tighter around her, nuzzling him with her cheek. "Do you think he knew?"

He didn't reply for a long moment. "He would have scented it in your blood. I think he knew."

Thirty-two weeks later their cub was born, a son with his father's eyes and mother's hair. And when the year and day was over, Terrence accepted their vows as husband and wife as well as mates.

IF YOU ENJOYED THIS STORY, YOU MAY ENJOY ...

CLAN CONROY BRIDES: 3 BBW Bear Shifter Romances

LIAM'S BRIDE: Curvy Meredith is hiding in plain sight. A gardening teacher for troubled teens, she needs the new owner of the old YWCA building to renew her lease. Alpha Bear Liam doesn't know his mate is the daughter of his father's killer. When he discovers her deception, will he reject her... and their baby? *(Chapter One Sneak Peak up next.)*

ALPHONSO'S BABY: Bear shifter Alphonso shunned his curvy mate Tamar to protect her from his dark past... but when he discovers he is the father of her baby, will he take the risk in order to raise their child?

NORELLE'S BEAR: A rebel Alpha billionaire. A beautiful, exiled Bear. A chance at love... but only if they break the Law. Exiled to Seattle until she drags home a rebellious billionaire to face the Council, Norelle discovers a possibility for love and family... but only at the expense of her future position in the Council.

LIAM'S BRIDE SNEAK PEAK

CHAPTER

1

Meredith sank to her knees, plunging her hands into moist earth. Closing eyes the same shade as the frothy carrot tops in her basket, she inhaled astringent sunshine and leafy greens. It steadied her, soothed nerves blasted raw by the call from the penitentiary earlier.

"Meredith?"

She pushed aside the Director's pained voice, wet seeping through the knees of her jeans. She didn't care. It anchored her to the present, reminding her why she hadn't left this small town and the troubling memories it held from her childhood. Memories courtesy of the person locked up over one hundred miles away- though not anymore. Her chest squeezed. He wasn't locked up anymore.

"Meredith!"

The snap in Sheane's voice jerked her out of a spiral of panic. Meredith blinked, feeling the blast of afternoon warmth on her cheek, wondered where she'd left her wide brimmed hat. Teenagers laughed several feet away, the tone of one sulky voice warning her she'd have to intervene in a moment or lose an entire crop of carrots. That girl used any weapon at her disposal to defend herself. Even an innocent urban garden.

Meredith looked up. "Sorry, Sheane."

The Director's brow furrowed, thin lines marring the natural beauty of large, loamy eyes. Meredith always thought Sheane belonged somewhere tropical and exotic- somewhere not a small city in Washington, surrounded by apple orchards and coyote and dense stretches of forest preserve.

"I can feel you're... upset, Meredith. But this isn't a problem that can't be solved."

Meredith laughed. One of her after school students glanced over, alerted. She altered the tone of the laugh. Protect the children. They had enough stress in their lives, they didn't need hers. She was sometimes the only island of calm among the adults they dealt with.

"I don't have the funding to solve this problem," Meredith replied, fingers twisting viciously in the soil, ripping handfuls of weeds from the roots. "If the new owner plans on converting this place into a culinary school- a werebear culinary school, then where does that leave us?" As lunch? She had plenty of meat on her bones.

She surveyed the rows of neatly cultivated plants in various stages of growth, shoulders slumping. Melons ready to pick, seedlings to prepare for the fall garden. Fluffy greens and vines of tomatoes so juicy people traveled from nearby towns to their farmer's market stall just for those, and the relish the kids prepared from the excess fruit.

Sheane sighed. "I understand and I wish there was something more I could do. I've explained to the new owner who the current tenants are, but he's adamant. Maybe you could try talking to him yourself. Your passion is contagious. It might help."

The slump turned to a hunch. Him. Ugh. She didn't want to talk to a him. She didn't want to go anywhere near a him who had the money to buy an entire building and convert it into a fancy cooking school. Especially if the him was... a Bear. Werebears were big, growly, and... just big. She'd avoided dealing with a big man since her father had gone to jail. Remembering why he'd gone to jail reinforced the reason she shouldn't have any contact with a werebear.

"I don't think that's a good idea."

Sheane shifted, the abrupt movement signaling her irritation. "Look, Meredith, I understand your issues. Believe me I do. The years I spent working at the women's shelter-"

"I'm nothing like those women," Meredith said, unhunching her shoulders. "I'm not... abused." The yelling, the anger her father inflicted on them during her youth she'd never tolerate from any man. And since most men had temper and ego issues- the bigger the man, the bigger his issues- she avoided them altogether.

Sheane said nothing for a moment. "Meredith..."

"I'll talk to him," she said, wiping the dirt off her hands. Rubbing it off. Dirt was dirt. It had no protective qualities. A movement caught her eye. She glanced past the teenagers, through the rough wood fence and into the parking lot. A car door slammed as a tall man walked away from a slick new SUV. A broad man, even from this distance. Dark hair and stern expression, strides eating pavement as he disappeared from view.

"That's the owner," Sheane said, following Meredith's view.

"It figures." No suit, but all that meant was he made enough money he didn't have to fit himself into an executive image. Kind of like a Mark Cuban.

"Why don't you go talk to him?"

She shook her head. "Not yet. I need time to think about what to say."

"Take time, Meredith," her friend replied, Meredith straining to hear her words. "But not too much time. Sometimes we have to push ourselves, even when we aren't ready. Otherwise you won't grow past your fears."

Meredith excused herself and went inside on the pretext of getting a glass of water. She sat in the worn chair of her tiny office after closing the door and pulling the blinds. The air conditioner worked this year, so the subtle chill iced the stress in her blood right away. Lowering her head onto her arms, she closed her eyes, focusing on her breath.

First problem, the call from her father letting her know the penitentiary released him on parole and he needed a place to stay. The awful frozen panic when she realized he wanted to come stay with her.

Inhale, exhale.

She wasn't a girl any longer, she was a grown woman. A grown woman with a life and friends and teenagers who depended on her. A role in the community. No one remembered whose daughter she was- not to look at her with anger or with pity.

A knock on the door forced her out of her dark reverie. Straightening, she called out. Brick walked in, too slender defiance in cargoes and an oversized flannel shirt. As if she were saying fuck you to the heat. Meredith's eyes zoomed in on her face. Second problem. Pain blossomed on the side of her cheek, vision going dark.

We don't play with Bears, her father roared. *Bears aren't safe. They aren't human.*

"Mere?"

Meredith forget her problems- shoved them to the back of her mind- rising to walk around her desk. "My God, what happened?"

Brick shrugged, pale eyes flicking over Meredith's shoulders.

"Fight. Just checking in cause I'm late."

Shadows marred the girl's face- bruising inflicted by multiple strikes.

"Do you want to talk to Sheane?"

Brick's lip curled. Meredith sighed. She sympathized. No one liked being labeled a victim- which talking to Sheane, a former domestic violence counselor, was almost like doing.

"Let's at least go to the kitchen and put ice on it." Meredith pushed with her hand on the door, something occurring to her. "Are you going to get in trouble with your case worker?"

"Only if someone reports it."

Meredith stared at Brick, who stared back, impenetrable as the nick name she'd chosen.

Meredith had learned the hard way not to call the girl Rebekah.

"And you don't expect the other person will?"

Brick smirked. Meredith grimaced. "Right. But you can't get into another fight. If you get caught-"

"Yeah, I know. Whatever."

Meredith waffled a minute, then sighed. "Let's go to the kitchen."

"There's people in there, you know."

She opened the door, stepping aside so Brick could precede her. "Oh? Well, we won't be long."

"Dudes. Big dudes."

Oh. Well, that was different. "Huh. Maybe we can-"

She caught the look on the teenager's face before Brick could disguise it under her usual half-bored, half-contemptuous mask.

Okay. Fine.

Meredith turned and marched down the hall, heading to the kitchen with Brick on her heels. They entered, Meredith poking her head in to look both ways. She heard a murmur of voices coming from the direction of the pantry. Good. They were going the opposite direction.

"Come on."

She led the girl to the industrial sized refrigerator, opening the freezer door and grabbing a bag of ice. She rummaged through supplies to find a plastic sandwich bag and measuring cup to scoop the ice- it wouldn't be nice to put bare hands over something others would drink later.

"Here," Meredith said, sealing the baggy and turning towards her student. "Put this on your face." She fixed Brick with a stern look. "Now, tell me what happened. You know you aren't supposed to get into fights, Brick. You could go back to the detention center."

"Only if you tell on me."

Leave it to a teenager to zoom in straight to the point. She knew she was obligated to report the incident, but she couldn't help feeling there was something more to it than Brick would say. Meredith had read the girl's file. The violent incidences in her past were precipitated by someone else attacking her, either physically or verbally. Brick never attacked first. Meredith didn't condone the use of force for verbal assaults- but no one had a right to put their hands on anyone else. Ever. So if the girl was defending herself against real harm, Meredith wasn't going to blame her.

Especially when she wished she'd been strong enough as a child to do the same.

* * *

"This is bullshit," Liam said, crumpling the letter in his hand.

Boden grinned at him. "They emailed a copy of the notice, too."

"You agreed to the lottery," Alphonso said, dark gold eyes calm. He leaned against a shelf, arms folded, long raven braid over a shoulder.

"I didn't think my name would get drawn," Liam growled.

"Stop whining." Boden said. "Find a hot human honey, settle down and have cubs, get hailed as a hero for bringing new genes into the Clan."

"You haven't seen some of the cubs born with the defects," Alphonso said.

Liam looked at him, attention reluctantly caught by the quiet gravity of his friend's voice. His resolve hardened. He'd seen the cubs, had just asked the parents to keep his visits on the down low. The Mother's Circle may have ended the bickering among the Nation about the best course of action to take, but that still didn't mean any perceived show of public support for this new, radical solution wouldn't stick in the jaws of some of the more vocal opponents. And he didn't need to lose precious time spent managing his business by arguing with his Den over his decision.

Too many cubs born in the last several decades with too many genetic defects caused by what boiled down to… inbreeding. Their Nation was small. It was rare to open the Den directory and not be able to find a relative, even a distant one. The best long term solution was to bring fresh genes into each individual Den to strengthen the Clans. Since he was not only Alpha of the local Den, but a member of the family that ruled Clan Conroy, he had a duty to set a good example.

Liam sighed. "What were the goddamn chances? Only ten males per Den drawn from the pool. It was supposed to be a long shot." But he'd promised his mother that if his name was drawn he would comply. Be one of the ten males per Den required to find human mates, the sooner the better.

"Someone's here," Boden said, head turning towards the door. They were closeted in the pantry off the kitchen- mostly because it was stocked, they were hungry and it was as good a place as any to have a quick snack and a quiet conversation since the offices weren't yet cleaned out to prepare for the remodel.

"Relax," Liam said to his younger brother. It wasn't as if they were talking anything top secret, and as soon as werebears started popping up with human mates all over the country, the jig would be up. The occurrence of a Bear-human marriage was rare enough that the media would eventually take notice when there were several. "There are still groups renting space in the building- they have ninety days to vacate."

Boden pushed the door open a sliver, peering out into the kitchen. "Hey, it's women. Cute women."

"I said-"

"I heard you." He left the pantry, moving towards the women.

Liam's fingers itched to settle around his brother's neck. Always distracted by a female. And human females at that. He scowled and walked after him. Boden leaned against a counter, body angled towards two women staring at him.

"I'm Boden," his brother was saying. "You ladies must be on staff here."

Liam snorted. He grabbed his brother's shoulder. "Stop harassing the humans and come on."

He stopped speaking, inhaling. An elusive scent of lavender and... carrots tickled his nose. Beneath it something earthy, tantalizing and quintessentially female. Boden shifted slightly as Liam moved forward, looking down at the female now in his line of vision. He stared, forgetting ire as he met wide eyes the color of chopped herbs. Loose waves of achiote colored hair appeared natural. His fingers twitched. The woman tore her gaze away from his, looking back at Boden, her curvy body stiff as she backed away, grabbing the teenager.

"We were just getting some ice," she said in a low voice. "We'll get out of your way."

Liam stepped forward, Alphonso approaching behind him. "No problem, you weren't disturbing us. What's your name?"

Rosy lips thinning, she refused to look at him. "I'm Meredith. Program director of Teens and Greens."

"Meredith." He stuck out his hand, a silent demand. "I'm Liam. The new owner of this building."

Her shoulders hunched forward, a small tell she controlled instantly, but not before the drapey neck of her pinky tunic flowed around her ample chest, giving him the barest glimpse of smooth flesh. It hugged her body, deceptively modest but accentuating curves before covering her jean clad hips and bottom. The earthy scent sharpened, and Liam realized she was afraid of him. Was it because he was a man, the new owner... or a Bear? Or any combination of the three?

But she took his hand, raising her eyes to his with a suddenness that brought a curve to his lips. She was forcing herself to confront him.

"I know who you are."

She squeezed his hand, strength in the grip. His smile widened. He wasn't attracted to weak women. Especially weak human women. But what was he thinking? His Bear was reacting to her scent like she was a chunk of dripping honeycomb. Her attention shifted to the male behind him. He saw recognition flit through her eyes, but she addressed Liam.

"I'd like to talk to you about your plans for this building," Meredith said, attempting to pull away. When she tugged a third time, he let her go. Slowly. She twitched; he followed her, shoulders angling so he could lunge and catch her if she should try and flee him.

Liam forced his lip, rising in a snarl, to smooth. Hell. What was wrong with him? Even Bear females didn't allow the males to pick them off and walk away anymore. Well- at least not without the male guaranteeing her cooperation beforehand.

He released her and stepped back. Fresh air. Fresh air would help. "Call my office, the receptionist will set up time for you."

Liam made himself turn away, grabbing his brother by the arm and pulling him along. Every step felt as if he were pulling nails from his fingers. Boden watched him, more interested in Liam now than the women.

"I don't believe it," Boden said, expression half speculative, half incredulous.

Liam ignored the two Bears, striding out of the kitchen. They would follow.

"You were damn near quivering when you saw that female. Liam, get her number. Damn, man. Your Bear-"

"Shut up, Boden."

"See?"

Liam saw his brother's smirk out of the corner of his eye, deciding now would be a great time to tackle and pummel him to the ground. It had been a while; Boden was due for some punishment. "Alphonso, tell him."

Alphonso was looking back the way they'd come, eyes narrowed slightly.

"What is it?" Liam asked.

After a moment the male shrugged. "She comes into the bar sometimes- always hanging out with Tamar. That hair is hard to miss."

"I've never seen that color before. It's-" he cut himself off before he said 'beautiful.'

"Guess it won't be so hard for you to get over this prejudice you have against humans,"

Boden said, smug. "The Mother's will be pleased at how obedient you are."

Liam lunged. He was an Alpha. He was not obedient, even if coincidentally, one little human woman made his Bear stand up and roar. Alphonso caught him around the waist.

"The children," the quieter man murmured. They were outside by then, halfway across the lot from where a group of curious teens paused their work in the vegetable and herb garden to watch the men almost fight. Liam had enough time to approve the neatness of the rows and healthy looking plants before shrugging free of his friend.

"I am not prejudiced. I just don't want anything to do with a human female."

"No choice, now."

No, there wasn't was there? But damned if he would admit to Boden that he was right, and after a scent of Meredith, his fate didn't seem quite so bad anymore.

"What do they feed them?" Brick asked, staring after the three tall, wide men as they left the kitchen.

The one whose hand had enveloped Meredith's in an inescapable grip, night sky eyes fixed on her with the pitiless intensity of a carnivorous predator, made her nervous. She'd lost her breath for just a moment, a tingling low in her stomach when he inhaled, nostrils flaring and broad chest widening. She knew about werebears. And she knew Liam was Alpha of the local Den- the collection of closely related families that were a part of a bigger Clan. She'd made it her business to know after- Meredith pulled her mind away from her old guilt.

"They're born big," she said.

Brick glanced at her, alerted by the short tone. "You don't like them cause they're Bears, or cause that's the guy taking the building away from us?"

Meredith frowned. "How did you...?"

The girl snorted. "I have ears."

Sighing, Meredith made another ice baggy to swap when the first melted. The man wasn't what she'd expected. She'd read every newspaper article mentioning him for years, before graduate school and the program forced her to get a life. In her mind the picture of some dismissive executive had formed. Instead, a new age Henry Cavill type in a banded collar shirt, expertly frayed cargoes and leather sandals greeted her, staring at her as if she was lunch. Weren't new agers supposed to be happy pacifists? This male was too... dominant for pacifism, consistent with his Alpha status. The other men would be aggressive, but an Alpha- they were both protective and aggressive and unusually territorial.

"Well, I'll have a talk with him and see if we can stay here."

"I'll do reconnaissance. Don't go in blind."

"Uhh... thanks, but I think I can handle it."

Brick said nothing. Now Meredith had something else to worry about, a teenager already prone to trouble playing detective.

She pressed a hand to her stomach. It still hadn't settled, her mind forcing the image of the dark man behind her eyes, taunting her. Because for the first time in a while, she was attracted to a man. Attracted and afraid, years of her father's teachings she'd worked hard to reverse strumming her nerves. Wonderful. So when she spoke to him again- and from his abrupt withdrawal, she felt convincing him to let her teens stay in the building wouldn't be easy- she'd have to fight nerves, attraction and her instinctive fear of werebears in order to speak coherently. Best thing she could do was start practicing now.

CLAN CONROY BRIDES: 3 BBW Bear Shifter Novellas
2.99 or FREE w/ Kindle Unlimited

myBook.to/ClanConroyBride

Want FREE stories from Emma Alisyn?

Sign up for her mailing list and get instant access!

smarturl.it/HowlList

WANT MOAR?
CHECK OUT EMMA'S OTHER TITLES:
(Betcha can't read just one)

CLAN CONROY BEARS
Liam's Bride
Alphonso's Baby
Norelle's Bear

ROYAL BEARS
Bear Prince
Bear Princess

MATES OF THE FAE
Fae Spark

ALPHA WEREWOLF MATES
Mated to the Enemy Alpha
Taken by the Werewolf

STEPBROTHER SHIFTERS
What A Mate Wants

CONTEMPORARY BBW ROMANCE
The Bride's Contract

ABOUT EMMA

Emma Alisyn writes paranormal romance because teaching high school biology wasn't like how it is on television. Her lions, tigers, and bears will most interest readers who like their alphas strong, protective and smokin' hot; their heroines feisty, brainy and bootilicious; and their stories with lots of chemistry, tension and plenty of tender moments.

Connect with Emma at:

www.hardcandiespublishing.com

http://facebook.com/emmaalisyn

Printed in Poland
by Amazon Fulfillment
Poland Sp. z o.o., Wrocław

14297136R00112